Cricket

Chapter 1.

The Dwyer family had travelled a thousand miles for a much-deserved holiday. For almost a year, the family had gone through hell. Now they were free from their torment.

Kevin and Clara had met at a wedding reception and formed the perfect friendship. Within months, it blossomed into a relationship. Within a year they too were getting married. Their friends celebrating their unison at the same venue where they first met, and Life had been good for them. Kevin worked at the Canadian embassy in London, while Clara worked as a midwife at the local maternity hospital.

Clara longed for a child of her own and they were both thrilled when she discovered she was pregnant with their first child, Charlotte.

A beautiful little girl, content and happy with everything. Three years later, Clara became pregnant again. This time the pregnancy was different. Clara would have constant issues with eating and sleeping. This became stressful for both her and Kevin and they were concerned that it would transfer to their unborn child.

William was born safely, fit and well. He was the perfect weight and had full crop of bright blonde hair. Everything was well again. Their fears were gone, and their family life continued, until Clara began having odd and disturbing dreams.

They all centred around William.

She would take the children to the park. She would sit and watch them playing. Yet within the blink of an eye, William had gone. She would look around, but there would be no sign of him.

Clara would shout his name, time and time again, but would get no reply. Charlotte would join her mother in the search.

When asked, Charlotte simply replied 'one minute he was here, then he just vanished '.

They would search the playground, double checking everything. then they would hear his laughter coming from the tree line that surrounded the area. Clara would see his faint silhouette, walking amongst the trees. She would run towards him, with Charlotte following closely behind. On approaching the trees, they found nothing. But still they heard his laughter. Every time they changed position, he would be gone, and the laughter would be heard somewhere else. Eventually, they would clear the other side of the trees and out into open fields.

Clara hadn't seen scenery like this in a number of years, since Kevin and herself had visited the lake district. The only sound they could hear now was the wildlife. Something wasn't right. The park was on the outskirts of the town and Clara knew that there weren't fields like this in their area. They had been moved there by something, but what. In the distance she was able to see a small crop of rocks protruding out of the ground. Standing on top, was a small figure that Clara would instantly recognise as William. They would slowly walk towards him. As they did, the sounds they would normally hear had stopped. Now all they could hear was the infrequent chirping of insects.

As they drew closer, Clara had confirmation that the person standing on the rocks was William. But something wasn't right. There was no wind, but his bright blonde hair was moving and appeared to be darker than normal. She called his name. suddenly the insects stopped their chorus.

Williams head slowly turned towards Clara. His face obscured by dark objects. They were crawling all over him and Clara would let out an ear-piercing scream. This would wake her up.

Sitting up and gasping for breath, Clara would try to remember what it was she had seen, but vague though the dream was, she couldn't piece together anything of it. This dream continued for two months. Every other night, she would have the same dream. Every time, the dream ended exactly the same. All Clara could remember was that William would go missing and she would eventually find him.

A week after the dreams first started, Clara chose a time to tell Kevin about them. He sat, listened and tried to be a sympathetic ear. He had seen things on social media about dream analysis and wondered if there could be a meaning to her dreams. He then did something that clearly upset her. He suggested going to the doctors to see what they would be able to do. After many tears, Clara agreed to go.

On the morning of her appointment, William had woken feeling unwell and had been sick a few times. Clara and Kevin agreed to keep him off school until he felt better. It would mean that William would be joining her at the doctors. They pulled into a parking space and walked into the medical centre. William found it amusing. "the waiting room is full of old people ", he would chuckle to Clara. Although she also found it funny, Clara kept a straight face and simply placed her finger to her mouth and shushed him quiet.

After what felt like hours. The buzzer sounded and a light lit up against her doctor's name on the wall. She placed the numbered disc onto the reception counter and walked towards the doctor's office. She tapped on the door and pushed down on the handle. It swung open to reveal the beaming smile of Dr Powell.

Dr Powell had been Clara's doctor, since she was a teenager and had overseen both Clara's pregnancies and aftercare.

He welcomed her in and ushered her over to a chair. She sat down and lifted William onto her lap.

"Good morning Clara, and what can I help you with?" he asked.

Clara's face turned red, she felt silly for asking, but if it helped, she wouldn't have a problem with it. She took a deep breath and proceeded to tell him about the dreams, while William sat playing with Clara's phone.

Dr Powell surprised her. He sat there and patiently listened to Clara's dilemma, looking at her with sympathy. His hands folded and placed in his lap. After a few minutes of Clara describing the nightmares she faced every night, he sat back, scratching his head. He then leant forward and cupped his hands together.

"Clara. Although dreams aren't exactly a medical issue, there is research on dreams within the scientific community and in theory, there could be an explanation to what you are going through".

"so, you cannot help me?" Clara replied.

"not exactly. However, there are some places that could help you maybe understand or explain the dreams you are having".

He turned to his computer and began typing. Within seconds, the printer in the corner whirled into life and began printing.

Dr Powell extracted the paper and handed it over to Clara.

"what are these?" she asked.

"these are websites that you can go to that may help. This website here claims that you could have some unresolved desire or alternatively attachment to a situation or person that you are unable to obtain. It's worth checking out" he replied.

A few months after William was born, Kevin had noticed that Clara wasn't as committed to William as she was to Charlotte. He just put that down to possible post-natal depression or as his family stated once, that the first born is always the favourite. Clara just couldn't get attached to him.

Now, she wondered if this was the real reason.

Could her dream be related to her connection with William?

She wasn't sure. But non the less, she decided she would look into this and see if there is one.

"and how is little William?" Dr Powell asked.

Clara took her phone out of Williams hands "Dr Powell has asked a question William ".

He looked up at Clara, then looked directly at the doctor.

"I've been sick" he replied.

"oh. How long have you been feeling this way William?".

"Just today" he replied and started to cuddle up to Clara.

Dr Powell looked directly at Clara "do you mind if I take a few tests?"

Clara was a little confused as to why she would go there for herself and it turned to be about William. She pushed that thought away and wondered again if that was related to the dreams also.

"of course," she replied.

The doctor withdrew some instruments from a drawer and began to examine William. After a few minutes, he placed them back in the draw. "do you mind if I take a little blood? It's just to check for anything viral".

This now worried Clara. Her little boy could have something serious.

"yes of course. That's fine" she replied.

A few anxious minutes passed, and it was done. Clara didn't like needles. For the sake of their health, she was happy for it to happen.

The doctor placed labels around the vials and placed them in a bag.

"the results should be back in a few days" and placed the bag on the table.

Clara and William left and made their way back to the carpark.

She unlocked the doors, sat William in his car seat and sat down in the driver's seat and simply sat there staring out the window.

Thoughts cascaded through her mind. What was going to happen next? what would she do? Was it her or William? What should she tell Kevin?

These things, she decided, will have to be sorted when it comes to it. For now, she would get home with William and have a look at the information Dr Powell had given her.

Once home, William went to his room and played with his toys, leaving Clara downstairs on her own. She would call Kevin on his lunch break to fill him in on what happened at the doctors. She made herself a cup of tea and sat down in the living room and started looking at the printout. She lent under the coffee table and retrieved her laptop. Normally, it was used to help the children with their homework. But every once in a while, it would be brought out to help with booking their holidays and maybe the odd bit of online shopping. Kevin and Clara were not avid internet users and would use it for themselves rarely.

Once the laptop started, she opened the browser and began looking up the internet addresses. The first three all told her the same thing. It was possible that the connection between her and William wasn't strong enough and her dream was telling her that. A few gave different opinions, but Clara was certain, she had the answer.

She called Kevin and explained what had happened that morning. Kevin was positive and tried to reassure Clara, that all would be fine. He was very good at calming people down and easing their worries.

That wasn't going to be the case and three days later, the call from the hospital changed everything.

Chapter 2.

William was feeling better and had returned to school with Charlotte. Charlotte had spent the three days going to school on her own and enjoyed the privilege of not having her little brother tagging along. Kevin was happy. He felt that it would do her good to be more independent. She was going to secondary school in September and insisted that she walked. This would be the perfect opportunity for her. Now William was well again, she would have to walk with him.

Clara had just sat down with a cup of tea when the letter box rattled making her jump. The postman usually delivered around nine o'clock but must have been running a little late. She walked down the hall. A small pile of mail sat on the floor. An elastic band wrapped it into one neat tidy bundle. She picked it up and walked back towards the living room, rifling through each letter as she walked.

The phone rang, making her drop the mail onto the floor.

She quickly picked up the mail and grabbed the phone. Pressed the accept button and headed back into the living room.

The conversation was short. Clara placed the phone down on the coffee table and placed her head into her hands. After a few minutes, she picked up her mobile, accessed her messages and proceeded to write a message to Kevin.

RING ME ASAP! ITS ABOUT WILLIAM.

And pressed the send button.

She wasn't sure how long it would take Kevin to get the message or how long it would take for him to reply. So, she just sat there and cradled her cup and waited. Twenty minutes later her mobile phone started to ring. It was Kevin.

She had no time to say anything.

As she was bringing the phone to her ear, she could hear Kevin talking.

"what has happened to William?" she could hear him shouting down the phone.

Clara explained again about the trip to the doctors earlier in the week and that he took bloods for testing. The results had come back and that they want them to go to the hospital and discuss them.

Kevin was speechless and an awkward pause ensued.

After a moment Kevin replied, "when do they want us to go in?".

"they want us there at midday tomorrow".

"I will sort something with work and let you know when I get home".

"ok honey. I'm really worried".

"try not to worry. I will see you all when I get home. I need to go. We have a meeting starting in a moment".

"ok sweety" Carla replied, and she heard the receiver go down the other end.

Kevin hated having to rush a call, when Carla is worrying, but his job was important. Carla knew that. she also knew that when Kevin returned home, he would give them all a huge hug before they sat down for dinner.

Sure enough, Kevin returned home. Walked through the door, threw his bag and jacket onto the floor and searched for his family.

This was a daily occurrence. Charlotte and William would run and hide as soon as Kevin pulled into the driveway. Then it would be Kevin's job to search the house for them.

Today was different. The search was short and sweet. He walked into the living room to find Carla and the children, sitting on the sofa.

"hi guys!" he asked. He was greeted with silence.

He sat beside Clara and took hold of her hands.

"it will be fine. Please don't worry" he quietly said, and a tear rolled down her face and disappeared into the collar of her jumper.

Within minutes, things appeared to be back to normal. Clara and charlotte were in the kitchen preparing dinner. William had gone upstairs to play on his computer. Kevin had made a coffee and was sitting there watching the news as always. He was never really impressed with what was going on in the world and didn't really enjoy watching the news. But it became a habit over the years, part of his routine.

They sat and ate in total silence and Charlotte was the first to speak.

"so mum, what is it that William has?"

Clara shuffled a few peas to the far side of her plate and took a huge breath in and sighed.

Kevin looked across the table, directly into her eyes. "I can explain it, if you like."

"it's ok "she replied and cupped her hands and placed them onto the table.

"the doctor thinks William may have something called PML disease, which is something to do with his brain."

"oh" replied Charlotte. "is it serious."

They could all see the sadness in Clara's eyes.

"I'm not sure sweety. We are going to have to have some more tests done to find out if it is that and what can be done."

"I hope he will be ok." And Charlotte started to cry.

Kevin got up from his chair and walked round to Charlotte and put his arms around her.

"I'm sure he will be fine" He said.

The evening continued as it started. Silence had descended on the house. Charlotte had gone to her bedroom to chat with her friends on Facebook. William had also gone back to his room and was playing on his computer. He was constructing a new world and wanted to spend as much time on it as he could and would continue until he fell asleep and the controller fell out of his hands. This would signal Kevin or Clara to go upstairs, turn the computer off and tuck him into bed.

With both children fast asleep, Kevin and Clara huddled close together on the sofa and watched tv.

An hour passed. Clara shuffled round and faced Kevin.

"do you think William will be ok?" she asked.

Kevin looked back, smiled and picked up his phone. He opened the browser and typed in PML disease.

"it says that it's the rarest brain disease in the world, with only three known cases." He replied and instantly regretted saying anything.

Clara suddenly burst into tears. Now the harsh reality and seriousness of the situation had kicked in. Kevin invites her into his arms and with tears pouring down her cheeks, she takes hold of him and sobs into his shoulder.

"let us wait and see what the doctors say after they have looked at him, before we think of the worst".

He could feel Clara's head nod. A few sniffles later, she had stopped crying and they sat there in the dark cuddling each other.

Neither them or the whole family would realise, the rollercoaster ride they would be about to ride, was going to be so chaotic and strange.

The following day would reveal more about Williams condition and would give Clara a restless night.

The house was still. Kevin and the children were fast asleep. In the darkness, Clara laid in bed, staring at the ceiling. She was making shapes out of the patterns of plaster and constantly thinking about the tests William was about to endure and worrying about how they were going to cope during this time. She tried pushing the thoughts aside and started to think of the fun times the family had had, in a strange bid to tire her mind. She would think of the lovely holidays they had been on and the fun times they'd had. A little smile appeared on her face and the silliest of thoughts appeared in her mind. 'what was going to happen about their holiday this year? They will have to cancel it'.

It was mid spring, and the weather was warming up, flowers were starting to sprout and bloom. The time of year when the children would start to spend more time outside and they would start looking at places to go on their holiday. Even the insects had started to appear.

With the better thoughts floating through her imagination, she fell asleep.

No sooner had she closed her eyes, she found herself back in the park. Only this time, something was different. It was hot and the sun was beaming down.

This dream was slightly different in that, William had already disappeared and Charlotte and herself were already looking for him.

They had already cleared the woods and were staring down at the rolling hills. She could see the pile of rocks and William standing at the top, motionless and staring out at the landscape before him.

The sound of crickets and insects were chirping loudly. The sound was increasing in volume. As Clara walked closer, the noise would get louder, until it was almost unbearable. She could see the bugs crawling over Williams body. They were coming out from within the rocks. In unison, they all walked in one direction. To his head. Clara couldn't see any bugs walking back down to the rocks.

She called out to William. Her voice echoing unnaturally.

As before the chirping of the bugs stopped. William began to turn around. As he did, the bugs stopped coming from the rocks, making it clearer for Clara to see where they were going. As William turned to face her, she reeled in horror.

The bugs were indeed walking up William and not walking back down again. The reason she could see. They were all entering his mouth and vanishing inside William.

Clara's mouth opened to scream, but no sound would come out. She drew another breath and tried again. Still no sound. Then she noticed a small line of bugs making their way from the rocks towards her. Like an army of ants marching towards food, they approached her.

She tried another scream and still there was nothing. The insects drew closer still. Now Clara was able to see them clearer. They were grasshoppers or crickets. She wasn't sure. Entomology was not her best subject school. But they had six legs and to her, they were horrible and creepy.

She drew one more deep breathe. As she was about to scream out, a voice came out from the trees. it was Kevin.

"Clara! Clara! He shouted out.

Clara may not have been able to scream, but she could still move. She turned to face the treeline and standing there in amongst a small clump of young saplings, was Kevin and Charlotte. Charlotte was waving frantically at her.

Confusion had now set in. she had a decision to make. Would she run to William and try to get him to safety, or run towards Kevin and Charlotte? The bugs by now had started to crawl up her legs. She could feel their tiny, pointed feet embedding themselves into her legs.

She realised there was no chance of saving William, so she ran directly to Kevin.

She brushed away the bugs as she ran, scattering them to the floor.

Clara's voice returned and as she called out to Kevin, a voice came from inside her.

'Mummy! Mummy!'

Kevin was still standing at the tree line calling out to her.

'Clara! Clara!

In shock, Clara stumbled and sprawled face first towards the ground. Before she could make contact, knowing what the result would be, she woke.

Kevin was standing by the side of the bed, gently shaking her and calling her.

She sat up, staring into Kevin's eyes. "I'm ok."

"are you sure? You seemed to be having quite a nasty dream." He replied.

Clara let out a small sigh and turned her gaze to the window. The sun had started to rise, and the birds had already started their dawn chorus. Somewhere in the distance a cockerel was crowing.

"I'm fine. Just had a bad dream that's all."

Kevin was curious. He knew about the other dreams but didn't want to pressure her into telling him what it was about. So, he just got himself dressed and went downstairs and made a start on the breakfast. Minutes later the children were up and ran down to Kevin in the dining room. Clara could hear their laughter, as Kevin would play around pretending to be the chef from the Muppet show.

She rose out of bed, put on her dressing gown, slipped into her slippers and made her way to the kitchen.

She grabbed herself a small plate and walked into a cheerful dining room.

Laying on the table, lay a wonderful spread of food, neatly arranged around probably what Clara thought was the biggest bowl of fruit salad in the world. She could smell the bacon and eggs cooking as she walked through to the kitchen.

She grabbed a knife and fork and started loading her plate and sat at her place at the table.

Both William and Charlotte were still giggling from whatever silly things Kevin had been doing earlier. Or so she thought.

This was beginning to make Clara a little suspicious. It was incredibly rare for Kevin to go to such lengths at breakfast time. This usually happened when Kevin had had a great idea, or he had won something exciting. The last time it had happened, he had been left a substantial amount of money from a rich uncle. Kevin hadn't seen him in almost twenty years when his mother called to tell him the news.

He was saddened by this information, but almost instantly knew what he was going to do with the money and within weeks, the deeds to their house had arrived from the building society. The house was now theirs, lock stock and barrel.

Clara could still picture the expression on Kevin's face when the paperwork arrived.

She wasn't sure what to say. She cut a piece of bacon and placed it into her mouth and began chewing. As she did, she glanced around the table. They all seemed happy with something. Clara knew not what, but she was intent on finding out.

After a few moments chewing, she swallowed the food, placed her knife and fork down beside her plate and picked up her coffee.

Now she was wondering what to ask Kevin. The children knew. They were in on his little secret.

A minute passed and she placed her mug down.

Chapter 3.

"Am I allowed to know the secret?" Clara asked.

The children both stopped, looked at Kevin and then back to Clara.

Kevin just sat there with a beaming smile on his face.

"I have an idea to run pass you, before we can set anything in stone." He replied.

"like what?"

"wait until the kids have gone to school and we can discuss it better then."

Clara was a little relieved. it didn't seem as serious, as she first thought and continued to eat her breakfast.

A short while later, they were all finished. The children were upstairs getting dressed. Clara was standing in the kitchen preparing their packed lunches. William was always picky with his sandwiches. It had to be a certain type of bread and it always had to be cheddar cheese. No other filling could be used.

Charlotte on the other hand, would eat whatever they placed in the lunchbox. In fact, she was almost as demanding. She would have to have a different filling every day. She loved her cheese and onion crisps, so they would have copious amount of them in a box in the pantry. Within moments of their bags being ready and sitting by the door, they came running down the stairs and into the kitchen.

Clara sighed "be careful."

Both immediately stopped. "sorry mum." Charlotte replied.

"you have to be gone in five minutes, go get your shoes on."

"ok." And they disappeared into the hall.

Clara looked up at the clock on the cooker. It was eight thirty. their bus would arrive in ten minutes. She turned to walk towards the hallway and the children. Kevin was standing in the doorway.

"I'm popping out the back for a few minutes" and he walked out to the garage. He would spend quite a bit of time out there lately, he would say it was a little project he was doing, and she wasn't allowed to go and peek. 'The garage is a man's domain' she thought, laughing to herself as she approached the children.

She gave them each a kiss on the cheek and politely directed them out of the door. She would watch them walk down the footpath, out onto the street and watch them until she couldn't see them anymore. The school bus drove directly past the house. When each of them first started at the school, Clara wouldn't close the front door until the bus had driven past and she had seen them sitting there.

Now they were a little older, she could trust them a lot more than she used too. So, with the door closed, she walked back into the kitchen, grabbed her mug, poured another cup of coffee and walked out into the back garden.

She could hear Kevin in the garage. Things were being moved around. There would be the clatter of things hitting the floor and then dragging sounds. As she grabbed the handle to the side door to the garage, the phone started ringing. Cancelling her plan to make Kevin jump, she released the door handle and walked back to the kitchen, to answer the phone.

She placed her mug down, walked over to the phone. She paused a little before picking up the handset and pressed the accept button.

"hello!"

"good morning! Is this Mrs Dwyer?" came a voice from the other end.

"yes, this is she!" Clara replied in her posh telephone voice. Clara and Kevin would always laugh about how they conducted themselves on the phone when people they didn't know would call them.

"ah, good morning. This is Doctor Parker from St Barts hospital. We have been given your son William's test results from your GP."

"hello Doctor Parker." She replied.

"Is it confirmed? Is it PML?" Clara asked.

"we think we can be pretty certain that it's the case Mrs Dwyer. Please understand that this is an extremely rare condition, with only three known cases in the world."

"ah ha, we have read up a little about it."

"so, you know there will be a long process ahead, to determine the next course of action and treatment."

"yes, we do." She replied, feeling a lump swelling up in her throat. Suddenly she felt like she had got to the climax of the saddest movie she had ever seen, when the lead character, that everybody loved dies.

She could feel the sadness welling up. She took a deep breath to try and calm the feeling. This was going to be the start of so much emotional turmoil for them all.

"are you ok Mrs Dwyer?"

"yes, I'm fine. So, what do you want us to do now?"

For a moment, there was silence. Clara stood waiting for the reply.

The next thing she heard, made her drop the phone. The reply she was waiting for didn't arrive. Instead, what sounded to Clara like crickets chirping came through the headpiece. While the phone sat on the floor, the sound grew louder, then ceased.

Clara couldn't believe what she had heard. It definitely wasn't the Doctor. She reached down, grabbed the phone and held it back to her ear.

"hello. Doctor Parker! Are you still there?" she called out.

She was calling out to no one. The phone was dead. Clara placed the phone back in the cradle and walked to the kitchen. As she turned into the doorway. She screamed as she walked directly into Kevin. His arms opened and stopped her from falling to the floor. His regular smiling face had turned to one of concern.

"are you ok sweety?" he asked.

"who was that on the phone?"

Clara wrapped her arms around him and pushed her head into his shoulder.

"it was Doctor Parker from the hospital. They are pretty sure it's that PML thingy" she mumbled through Kevin's jumper.

She felt embarrassed about the cricket sounds and the dropping of the phone, so she attempted to hide it from him. Only Kevin's next question forced her to reveal what happened.

Clara didn't realise that Kevin had been there since she answered the phone. He was standing in the kitchen within earshot of her conversation with the Doctor. He listened in to the point where she dropped the phone.

"how did you drop the phone?" he asked.

She looked shyly at Kevin. She didn't want to reply, but she knew she had no choice.

"it was the crickets again" she finally replied.

"the crickets? What the ones from your dreams?".

"yes."

"I was talking to Doctor Parker. Suddenly, he went quiet and then the sound of crickets came down the phone."

Kevin was shocked. He could understand the dreams, but now, these dreams had pierced into reality.

"what can this mean?" he asked.

"I don't really know, but it has something to do with William."

Clara picked up the phone and redialled the last number received. A few rings passed.

"hello. Doctor Parkers office. How can I help?" came the voice at the other end.

"Hello, I was just speaking with Doctor Parker about my son William."

"of course, Mrs Dwyer. I will put you through now."

There was a slight musical interlude, a click. Then the next thing Clara heard was Doctor Parker.

"Hello Mrs Dwyer. I'm not sure what happened there. The phone just cut out."

"I'm not sure either. But had some weird noises coming down the phone instead of you."

"strange. Anyway Mrs Dwyer. Is it still ok for Mr Dwyer and yourself to pop into my office at midday?"

"midday will be ok?"

"wonderful. I will see you then."

"ok Doctor Parker. Thank you."

She could hear the sound of the crickets again, the same as before. Clara called out down the phone "goodbye!" and quickly put the phone down. she didn't even wait for an answer.

She turned to face Kevin. "let's go and chat. I have a plan." Said Kevin.

Clara sat down at the table and Kevin went into the kitchen and poured two more mugs of coffee.

Moments later, he returned to the dining room. Sat down next to Clara and slid her mug over to her.

"so, what is your plan?" Clara asked. "has it got something to do with what you were doing in the garage earlier?"

Kevin smiled. "of course, it has."

He proceeded to explain his plan.

It was all dependant on what Doctor Parker would suggest at the meeting. Clara sat and listened. The idea would be that, before Williams treatment would start, they would go away for a holiday. Everyone would then be nicely relaxed.

"all we need to be sure of, is to check the school is ok with it."

Clara smiled. "I can't, see the school having a problem with it, but I will go and talk with them after we have seen Doctor Parker."

They both walked upstairs to freshen up and get dressed. They had a couple of hours before they needed to be at the hospital, so, they both agreed they would go and do some shopping first.

With the shopping done, they drove to the hospital. Parked the car and walked into the paediatrics department.

The whole department had been upgraded and was gleaming and bright.

They both walked to the reception desk hand in hand. Upon their approach, a head popped up from behind and gave Kevin and Clara a beaming smile.

"how can I help you?" she asked.

Kevin smiled back, "yes, hello. We have an appointment to see Doctor Parker" and he looked at his watch. "in ten minutes" he followed.

The receptionist looked at her screen, squinted a little, then smiled again. "ah yes, here we are. Mr and Mrs Dwyer?"

"yes, that's right" Clara replied.

The receptionist typed into the computer and held her hand up, pointing to the waiting area seating.

"if you would like to take a seat. I will let Doctor Parker know you are here."

"thank you" Kevin replied and they both turned and walked over to the seats.

Clara was feeling nervous and it showed. Kevin was too, but he was trying to be strong, not just for himself, but also for Clara and the children. He was as scared for William and he prayed constantly that everything would be ok.

As they sat and waited, neither of them really felt the need to talk and they sat in an awkward silence. Kevin was browsing through a copy of the people's friend, while Clara would just sit there looking around. Every now and then, she would look and see what Kevin was reading.

Then something rang in her ear. No one around her reacted, not even Kevin, who was sitting next to her. It was no ordinary ring and she sat there trying to place where she had heard it before. The sound only lasted a mere second, but it was enough to get her attention. Then she realised what it was that she had heard. It was the sound of a cricket.

'where the hell has that come from' she thought, and she started to look around the waiting room.

Clara suddenly stopped looking. Her eyes transfixed at the window.

The paediatrics centre was based in the heart of the hospital and was designed as an enormous square with a large open quad in the centre. It was normally open to the public to sit in while they waited to be seen. But today, it was closed while a couple of electricians were in to install a speaker system. Some of the patients and visitors had complained that they enjoyed sitting out in the fresh air but couldn't hear their names being called. The hospital trust decided that the speakers would be a great idea.

At first, Clara thought it was probably one of the workmen. And she started to look away. As she started to move her head, she noticed something on the windowsill. Her eyes focused. What she saw, made her jump out of her chair and grab Kevin's arm. This in turn made him jump.

"what the hell!" he called out.

Clara pointed to the window. Her finger shaking "look!"

Kevin put the magazine down onto the table and looked at the window.

Confused, Kevin stood up and walked towards the window. He wasn't sure what he could see and wanted to get a closer look.

As he got closer, the image grew clearer. He stopped and stared.

It was a cricket.

Slightly shocked, he turned to see Clara sitting with her hands over her face, her legs were trembling. He drew a deep breath and just as he was about to tell Clara what it was, the receptionist called out.

"Mr and Mrs Dwyer! Doctor Parker will see you now."

Clara shot up out of her chair with Kevin sprinting behind her trying to catch up.

Chapter 4.

They walked down a small corridor laced with bright blue doors either side. The floor was clean, pale grey and was inlayed with only what Kevin thought were crystals or glass. The walls had been painted in a brilliant white and scattered here and there were small posters advertising everything from the health service and the different departments, through to the shops at the main reception and what special deals they were offering.

At the far end of the corridor, facing them was Doctor Parker. He was standing in the doorway to his office, waiting to greet them.

As they approached, he smiled and held out a hand to Kevin.

"good afternoon Mr and Mrs Dwyer. Please come in" and he motioned them into his office.

They entered the small office. The walls covered with posters about personal health. A typical medical skeleton stood upright in the corner, suspended by a stainless-Steel arm. Next to that, was the

Doctors desk. It was covered with paperwork, books and folders. His computer quietly whirring away to the right of the desk.

They all sat down. Kevin crossed his legs and placed his hands on his knees. Clara sat straight with he hands on her knees, gazing directly at Doctor Parker.

Doctor Parker sat cross legged, did a quarter turn and picked up his pen.

He opened a file on his desk to reveal pages of writing and boxes of some sort. He clicked the mouse button and the computer screen burst into life. William's details appeared.

"ok, do you mind if I call you by your first names?" he asked.

"of course, please do" Clara replied.

Kevin just sat and nodded.

"thank you. Ok. This is where we are at the moment" and he proceeded to explain what PML was and how this may effect William and of course the whole family.

As soon as he started, questions started flowing through Clara's mind.

Kevin sat there motionless and speechless. In fact, he was actually in a state of shock. He couldn't believe this was happening to his son. His William. He isolated himself from everything. His spirit had left and gone elsewhere, leaving a lifeless, empty shell in the Doctor's office.

He wasn't too sure that his spirit wanted to be where it was now either. He was in total darkness. There was nothing. He couldn't see a thing. That was the only one of his senses that failed to work. He could hear birds chirping in the distance and the sea washing up on a shoreline. He knew he must be near the sea. He could smell food being cooked; a blend of cooked meats was floating in the air. He could feel warm, wet grass around his feet. 'I'm not wearing shoes?' he asked himself. Inside the darkness of his sub-conscious, he was checking himself. He was still wearing clothes albeit, not the clothes he was wearing at the hospital.

He was wearing shorts and a t-shirt. It was also hot. He could feel the heat in the air around him. Wherever he was, it certainly wasn't the Doctor's office.

The birds fell silent and Kevin stopped hearing the sea. Something had changed. Then he noticed even the smells had changed. Instead of the delightful smell of food. Now was a smell of decayed, rotten flesh. Suddenly a sound from the distance came towards him. Silently at first, then it grew louder. The darkness had now found a new voice, one that was starting to terrify Kevin. It was the sound of crickets.

He started to take a step backwards as the sound turned into a vision. Thousands of crickets slowly walking towards him.

He was about to scream out, as they arrived at his feet, when he heard Clara call his name.

With a flash of white light, he was back in the office.

"are you ok Kevin?" Clara asked as she took hold of Kevin.

His vision was slightly blurry. As it cleared, he saw Doctor Parker holding some tissue out in front of him. While Kevin was receiving this vision, he was totally unaware of what was happening around him. He wasn't sure of what was happening where he went in this nightmare. Then he remembered how hot it was and lifted his hand to his face. He was sweating. Kevin reached forward and took the offered tissue, sat back and wiped his face.

Clara was wearing the face of concern. "are you ok Kevin?"

"yeah, I think so."

"you were miles away there" replied the Doctor.

"I'm not sure what happened there, but I'm ok."

He sat back and took a few deep breaths to calm himself down.

"are you sure?" Clara begged. She knew something wasn't right. The turn of events earlier had scared her enough and this was now on another level.

"I'm fine" Kevin replied sternly. "must be stress."

He held Clara's hand and looked into her eyes. He mouthed the words "honest I'm fine" and nodded.

He turned to face Doctor Parker again. "it's ok. Carry on."

Doctor parker placed both hands in his lap "if you are sure."

Kevin nodded.

"after the tests we carried out, it looks like he may have something called PML. I won't give you the full name as it will probably take me all afternoon to pronounce it."

"what is it basically" Clara asked.

"we are not quite sure at the moment and we will need to do further tests. Unfortunately, they may be fairly intrusive. But basically, it's a viral infection of the white matter in the brain. At the moment its mild so we will need to monitor it after the confirmation tests and treatment"

"treatment? Does that mean you can cure it?" Kevin pleaded.

"Because we have detected it fairly early, we should be able to treat it successfully, but this virus can be fatal, hence the extra tests."

"what sort of tests?" Clara replied.

"unfortunately, we will need to take a cell sample."

"you are going to cut his head open?" Kevin shouted.

Doctor parker raised both hands "no Kevin. We don't need to do that. all we need to do is drill a tiny hole through the skull bone to get access to the infected cells. We will then take a small sample of damaged cells and then put everything back, the way it was."

Kevin had heard what the Doctor had said, but it didn't matter. By now his head was in the palm of his hands and sobbing into them. His little lad was in serious trouble and was totally unaware of the danger he was in.

"please Kevin, Clara, he will be fine through this procedure. The sample will be taken from an area that won't leave a visible scar or damage him any further. The hole will be drilled in an area with hair."

"ah well, that's alright then isn't it."

Clara placed her hand on Kevin's lap.

"you know this has to be done. It's for Williams sake."

Kevin drew a deep breath.

"yeah, I know. But how does he get something like this virus? I have never heard of it until now. If it's a virus, why hasn't it infected more people?"

Doctor Parker turned his chair, to face his computer. He typed in a couple of words onto the keyboard. The screen flashed and displayed pictures and paragraphs of writing.

He turned back. "ok. This virus originates from something that is very common in most people. Eighty five percent of the adult population has the original virus. The PML virus comes from that."

"the original virus?"

"yes. The original virus is called the John Cunningham virus. Most of us are infected by it in childhood. So, it is very strange and rare for the virus to turn into the PML strain."

Kevin had stopped sobbing and had composed himself. The whole situation was terrifying him, but he had pulled himself together and was now concentrating on what the Doctor was saying.

"so, with the treatment, William should be able to make a full recovery?"

"I don't see any reason why not. I think we have caught it in the early stages, but the biopsy will confirm this."

"so, when do we need to come back for tests?"

Doctor Parker opened the diary on the computer "we can have William in on Wednesday next week at nine in the morning."

They both looked at each other. Kevin spoke first. "I can book off work, the boss will be fine with it."

"it's ok. You go to work. I'm home that day anyway and I can keep you updated" Clara replied.

Clara turned back to Doctor Parker "that's fine, 9am it is then."

"please don't worry, I'm sure it will all work out for the best."

"thank you, Doctor."

With that, both Kevin and Clara stood up from their chairs. Kevin extended his hand.

"thank you, Doctor" and shook his hand before heading towards the door.

"yes. Thank you. William and I will see you next week" Clara added.

The doctor did a side nod gesture and smiled.

"you're welcome. If you think of any other questions, please don't hesitate to contact either the reception or directly to this office" and he handed Clara a small card with his contact details on.

"thank you" and Clara joined Kevin at the door.

Moments later, they were sitting in the car. They just sat there looking out of the windscreen. The keys were in the ignition, but Kevin didn't want to start the car. He simply wanted to wait a moment in silence.

"are you ok?" Clara asked.

"yeah!" Kevin replied and the car whirred into life and soon they were on their way home. The conversations varied, from what they were going to have for dinner, to where they were going to go on their holiday.

The holiday was a short conversation. A few ideas were mentioned, but Clara wanted to get the tests out of the way first before they decided what to do and stopped the subject.

After a short while they were close to the children's school.

"Kevin! Can we stop at the school and have a chat with the head teacher about William?" Clara asked.

"good idea. At least then we will know if we can have the permission" he replied and the pulled into the school car park.

The school car park was only small and provided spaces for the forty staff and ten spaces for visitors. It sat to the side with a small pathway that led round to the front where the entrance to the reception was situated.

The entrance was neat and tidy and was decorated in a crazy but modern fashion. Kevin was quite amused by the sight. He had joked with Clara about it before, during a parents evening. He thought that the headteacher had given the children, various amounts of different coloured paints and let them loose on the building. There were multicoloured blotches on the floors, walls and ceilings. Even the chairs and counters were of different colours than normal.

They walked in through the doors and approached the reception counter.

There didn't appear to be anyone in. Kevin and Clara looked at each other and laughed. "it would appear, that there is no-one home" Kevin quipped.

Suddenly, they both jumped as a beady eyed face, popped up from behind the counter. They both laughed and smiled at the receptionist.

"can I help you?" she asked. her voice was as beady as her stare. Squeaky and rattled. Kevin amused his mind further 'she must be a sixty a day habit.' He thought.

Then he gasped, as his thought was near enough confirmed. She picked up a pen from the counter, revealing her tobacco-stained fingers. They were an almost golden brown from decades of the habit. Kevin knew better not to comment, although he wished he could. He was finding it quite repulsive to look at. Every time he would look away, he would find his gaze return to her hands.

"yes, we would like to speak to Mr Ford, the head teacher please." Clara replied.

"I will see if he was available. Can I have your names please?" "it's, Mr and Mrs Dwyer "Kevin replied. She leant over and picked up the phone. After a few moments she spoke to someone at the other end, hung up the phone and returned her gaze towards Kevin and Clara.

She leant forward. Again, Kevin's eyes were again transfixed on her hands.

"someone will be down in a moment" and she raised her hand gesturing to the psychedelic seats behind them.

They both wandered over to the far end of the reception area and sat down. Kevin couldn't resist and turned to Clara. "did you see the state of her fingers?" Clara sniggered. "yes, but don't let her hear you say that" and they both sat with a small fit of the giggles. They're fun stopped, when a side door opened, and a small round head popped through the doorway.

"Mr and Mrs Dwyer?" He called.

They instantly stopped laughing and rose out of the seats. They approached the door. Kevin was the first to raise his hand to greet the head in the doorway, which swung all the way open to reveal a smallish man in his early fifties. He reminded Clara of Captain Manwaring from Dad's army. His rounded glasses were three times the size of his eyes. The reception lights were creating a gleam on his bald head. As he spoke, Kevin had to rely on his inner strength not to fall to the floor laughing. "hello. I am the head teacher, Mr Ford" in a loud booming voice. As he spoke, a rather large bag of skin under his jaw rattled from side to side. Luckily for Kevin, he pulled himself together by looking at Clara. She knew what Kevin was thinking. Although she too, found it amusing. Her inner strength was a lot stronger than his. With a returning glance, Kevin was able to resist temptation and kept himself calm and held his hand out to greet Mr Ford.

"pleased to meet you Mr Ford" Kevin replied. Clara stepped forward.

"hello, Mr Ford. We would like to speak to you about Charlotte and William. Mainly about William though."

"of course. Please follow me." And he waved his hand down the corridor, directing them to his office.

As they walked, Kevin started to whistle the Laurel and Hardy theme tune quietly to which Clara gave him a sharp jab in the ribs.

Kevin winced as she made contact and followed it with a smile and a giggle. Clara put a finger to her mouth "shh, not now" and smiled.

Within moments, they were standing at his office doorway. Strange ornaments decorated everything inside. Bizarre pictures hung on the walls, similar to that in the reception. On his desk were odd, shaped objects made of wood and clay and strangely decorated in pieces of fabric and other materials. There was definitely an art themed presence in the school and Kevin believed that was a key part of the motivation for the children.

"please sit!" Mr Ford directed. Kevin and Clara sat down and made themselves comfortable.

"would you like some tea or coffee Mr and Mrs Dwyer?"

Kevin was pleasantly shocked. He had never been asked that before, even when the annual parents evening took place. He had the general conception that most schools didn't waste money on things like that for a five-minute conversation with a teacher or principle.

"that would be lovely, thank you" Clara replied.

Mr Ford picked up his phone and dialled through to the reception.

Within minutes, there was a knock on the door and the receptionist entered with a tray. She placed it down on the desk. Kevin let out a snigger. He found it amusing that there in the centre of the tray, was a small plate of biscuits. But they weren't just any biscuits, they were Kevin's favourite, hobnobs.

"help yourselves to milk, sugar and a biscuit or two" and he passed the plate to Clara. She accepted the plate, took a biscuit and passed it to Kevin. He took two and placed the plate back on the tray and retrieved a mug of coffee.

Mr Ford took a careful sip out of his mug. "before we start, please call me Max. I like to be on first name terms with people, it doesn't sound so strict."

"of course," Clara replied.

"lovely. So, what can I help you with?"

Kevin was busy dunking his hobnob into his mug, so, Clara took hold of the conversation.

"we have just recently been given the news, that William has a rare virus."

Max's eyebrows raised. He put down his mug and clasped his hands together. He was showing great concern.

"do they know what it is?"

Kevin placed his mug back on the tray. "it is something to do with his brain. They need to do more tests" he added.

"yes. We have a set of tests to do next week, to determine what steps to take in regard to treatment."

Mr Ford suddenly surprised Kevin and Clara. "of course, if you need William to have time off. Then of course, that will not be a problem."

There was a slight pause. Kevin reached down and took hold of Clara's hand and held it close.

"we are not sure yet on how serious this situation is. But what we are wondering, is, would we be able to take William and Charlotte out of school for a holiday before he starts the treatment."

Max's eyebrows raised again. He looked sympathetic. "That will be no problem. Any time you guys need off, just let us know when and we will sort it out. These are exceptional circumstances."

"thank you." Clara replied. "yes, thank you. As soon as we know what's happening, we will contact you." Kevin added.

With the meeting ended, Kevin and Clara left Mr Fords office and made their way back to the car.

Chapter 5.

As they sat in the car, Kevin glanced at his watch and noticed that the children would finish school for the day in ten minutes. So, they just sat and waited.

After a couple of minutes of silence, Clara opened her door. "I will go and wait for the children to come out."

"ok sweety" he called back as she walked away. As he sat alone, he decided to listen to some music and switched the radio on.

Clara walked briskly to the main entrance where the children would exit the school to make their way to the buses. She leant against the railings like a customer would at a bar waiting for a drink when the school bell went. Seconds later followed by the exodus of screaming children exiting the school. Children, coats and bags flying in all directions made it difficult for Clara to see William and Charlotte. Her gaze going in every direction to pinpoint her children.

After a moment, the exodus had calmed down and only a few stragglers remained. Just as the last of the children had got on the buses the reception doors opened and out came William and charlotte side by side.

Clara felt proud that her two children got on well together, they never really argued or bickered and as Charlotte knew about Williams condition, she showed a bit more care towards him. As soon as they saw Clara, they both smiled and ran towards her. As soon as they were a few feet away, William dropped his bag and ran at full steam into Clara's arms. Charlotte just calmly walked to her side.

"Hiya kids. Are you okay?"

From the side of Clara's hip, she could hear a muffled voice.

"yeah!" William replied.

They walked back to the car where Kevin was not paying attention to his surroundings and playing air guitar and miming to songs on the radio. He almost flew through the sunroof when Clara banged on the side of the door. In a flash Kevin switched off the radio and adjusted his posture in the seat, in a strange attempt to hide his embarrassment which unfortunately for him was too late. Almost every parent and child that used the car park had seen every move Kevin had made.

"Well, that wasn't too embarrassing, was it dad?" as the passenger door opened, and Charlotte crashed into the back seat.

William sat down in his seat and placed his seatbelt over his shoulder, then clicked it into place. "They will take the micky out of us for weeks because of that. Thanks a lot dad!" he added.

"ah, it's only a bit of fun" Kevin replied, and they headed off home.

As soon as they arrived home, the children threw off their shoes and coats and ran upstairs to their bedrooms, leaving Clara and Kevin to pick them up and put them away.

"It's ok, we will tidy up your mess" Clara shouted up the stairs and walked through to the kitchen. She switched the kettle on and proceeded to make herself and Kevin a cup of tea. She could hear the children moving about upstairs.

William had made himself comfortable on his games console, which he played every afternoon after school until dinner time. It would then be switched off and not be turned again until the following afternoon. Both of them knew that after dinner was homework time.

Charlotte had disappeared into her room and as always, she put on her music and just laid on her bed talking to her friends on Facebook. She never felt the need to play games. The stage of boys was entering her life and that would be all that her and her friends would discuss.

Kevin had sat at the table in the dining room. Laptop in front of him.

Clara walked in and placed a cup of tea down by the side of the laptop and peered over his shoulder.

"what are you doing?"

"I'm going to have a look at some holidays. Where do you fancy going?" he replied clicking from one page to the next.

Clara had been to many places in her childhood. Her favourite had been Athens. She was twelve when her parents decide to spend two weeks in Greece. As Clara enjoyed reading historical books and showed considerable interest in the Acropolis. They had decided on to go there. She was in her element. Clara would visit bookstores and buy books on the history and treasures of ancient Greece and particularly Athens.

She idolised the pictures of the ancient statues and structures and placed posters about her bedroom. Her mother and father praised her many times for her interest and would buy her more books and posters if they came across any. The holiday was the best. They toured all over Athens. The old Olympic stadium, the acropolis and many temples. Clara didn't want to return home. Now those memories came flooding back to her once more.

"how about Greece?"

Kevin typed Greece into the search engine. Within seconds page after page of holidays sprawled into view on the screen. He clicked on the first holiday firm advertising cheap discount holidays to Greece and the Ionian islands.

"ok. Where do you want to go?"

"I'd love to see one of the islands" she replied.

Kevin giggled. "you do realise there are thousands of islands in Greece."

"I know. Maybe we should do a lottery."

"meaning?"

Clara's mind went into overdrive. "ok. We each pick three islands. Put them in the hat and draw one each, to make a short list. Then, we look at the remaining four and decide between us which one to go to."

Kevin loved the idea and walked to the side cabinet and took out a note pad and pen. He sat back down at the table.

"we are going to let William and Charlotte choose too?"

Clara shrugged her shoulders. "I don't see why not!" and she walked over to the living room doorway. "they are as much a part of this, as us." she opened the door and poked her head out into the hallway.

"Kids, can you come down here for a minute please?"

She walked back to the table and sat beside Kevin.

There was a faint rumble as both William and Charlotte burst into life and made their way out of their bedrooms towards the stairs. The rumble was faint to start with and as they came down, the rumble became louder. Then stopped as both of them thumped off the bottom step and into the hallway.

"yes mum" and Charlottes head peered in through the door.

Clara beckoned them in "please come and sit down" and motioned them towards them.

They both sat down, and Clara and Kevin began to explain what was going to happen.

William looked excited at the idea of going away for a few weeks.

Charlotte looked a little annoyed. She didn't want to go away. She wanted to stay at home and be around her friends. Once it was explained about William's condition and what he was going to have to go through. She changed her mind and they both began to tear off small pieces of paper from the notepad and began writing suggestions out.

Minutes later, their choices were complete. All the pieces of paper we folded up and placed in a small clear food bag.

The lottery was about to begin. Kevin shuffled the bag.

"ok. Each of us will take turns in pulling two tickets out of the bag. These are the choices that we will throw away. Then remaining four, will be the choices that we have to decide on."

William took the first pick and placed his on the table in front of him.

Then Charlotte, Clara and finally Kevin, leaving four pieces of paper in the bag. Kevin scooped the discarded paper into his hands and threw them into the wastepaper basket in the corner of the room. He then tipped the bag out onto the table and started to unfold the papers and lay them out.

Clara gasped as three of the four choices were identical.

"oh my god. How weird".

Kevin looked on, astonished at what he was seeing. On the table in front of them the papers read CORFU, CORFU, CORFU, CRETE.

Out of the possible choices there could possibly be, there seemed that a decision had already been made. They all turned and looked at each other.

"something wants us to go to Corfu!" Kevin remarked.

Clara picked up the papers out of the bin and unfolded them. She suspected that maybe the same island had been put down numerous times and as she viewed the papers, her suspicions were quashed. They had all picked Corfu as a choice. But many other islands had also been chosen.

Amazed by her findings, she placed them back into the bin and sat down.

"I think the majority has it and Corfu it is then." And picked up the papers and shuffled them in her hands. She was a little alarmed by what happened, especially after her dreams and experiences.

Kevin tapped the keypad and the screen changed. Pictures of Corfu appeared on the screen.

"Wow. That place looks cool!" William shouted and he started jumping up and down with excitement.

Kevin was scrolling through different images of the islands resorts.

"so, now we have where we are going. We just have to pick where on Corfu we go" and he continued scrolling through photos.

Clara liked the look of the island, so was happy with the choice, no matter how strange the choice had come about.

Kevin returned to his search engine home screen and typed 'holidays to Corfu'. He clicked on the first choice and their homepage whizzed into view.

Charlotte sat watching. Every now and then, she would type onto her phone. She couldn't resist chatting to her friends even though they were in the middle of a family meeting. Then her phone made a pinging sound and she return to looking at her phone and typing. Clara wasn't impressed and gave Charlotte a slight scowl. She put the phone down, stood up and walked up behind Kevin. "My Friend Sarah, says try Sidari."

Kevin opened up a separate page and typed the name in and clicked on images.

Both Kevin and Clara looked at each other. They both then nodded. "good choice Sarah and Charlotte" Kevin called.

"Sarah went there last year. She loved it. She says that there is something for everyone there." She replied.

They all stood behind the laptop, browsing through the pictures.

The first, was of the town centre. A traditional looking church, painted in cream and white stood out amongst streets full of tourists bustling in and out of shops, in search of bargains. Its bell tower watching over them.

Olive trees had been planted all around the grounds, providing shade to all that required it. Children were playing around a large bandstand placed in the centre and out to the rear, a children's playground could be seen under the over-hanging branches.

Clara's heart knew for sure, that, that was where they had to go.

The next few pictures were of the local beaches. They were relatively clean, with beautiful clear blue water.

Kevin went back to the previous page. His mind had been made up also. Sidari was going to be their destination.

"the question is, who do we go with A tour agent or go private?" Clara asked.

In the past they had done both. Kevin's opinion was that they were as good as each other. Clara felt that private apartments were better. She didn't like tour operators throwing day trips into their faces every day. She enjoyed just being allowed to explore at her own pace. A gift that was given to her by her parents.

She looked at the children. "what would you like to do guys? Do you want to go to a hotel or have an apartment?"

Both Charlotte and William looked at each other, laughed and said simultaneously "apartment!"

Clara laughed along. Kevin replaced his search with apartments to rent in Sidari, Corfu.

The children both went back upstairs and carried on with their activities. Kevin and Clara sat there for a while longer looking for different apartment complexes to rent.

There were hundreds to choose from. Most of the town was comprised of apartments. Only a few hotels existed there.

"we have a lot of choices to look at here" Kevin laughed and started browsing some more.

"to narrow it down, we want to be close to the beach but not too far from the town." Clara replied.

"that's good. That has taken over half the apartments out of the equation."

A thumping came from the hallway and Charlotte came bursting into the room. "mum, dad. Sarah has given me the name of the apartments they stayed at. She says they were amazing; they had their own pool, and it was really close to the beach." And she held up her phone.

On the screen was a picture of a pool surrounded by a beautiful garden. Green grass grew around the edges. Around the edges of the gardens, were a variety of olive trees and flowering shrubs.

"wow!" Kevin replied. "is that the place?"

"yeah. The beach is just down the road apparently and only a few minutes' walk from the town centre" and she started to type into her phone. "I will ask Sarah if she can remember the name of the place."

Within seconds, her phoned bleeped and she held the phone to her face.

"yes! She says the apartments are called Megali luxuries."

"righto, let's have a look." Kevin replied and he started typing.

He selected the website and then clicked on the section titled gallery. Clara gasped. "that place looks amazing! Let's go for that."

"if it is available. We have left it a little late to book" Kevin replied.

"you never know. We may get lucky."

He clicked on contact and proceeded to write a carefully worded email.

With a final click, the email was sent. "just a matter of waiting for the reply now." He shut the lid down and walked into the kitchen and started to make a cup of coffee.

Clara wanted to see more, so she sat down at Kevin's seat at the table and lifted the lid.

Starting at the beginning of the gallery, she flicked through the pictures. With everyone she saw, her love with the idea of Corfu grew inside her. After a moment, Clara stopped and looked in horror.

On the screen in front of her was the picture of a cricket. Bright green with long hind legs and looking directly at her. She shook her head and blinked a few times. She was frightened of the image and wanted it gone. When she opened her eyes again, it had. Now on the screen was an image of the swimming pool, taken from one of the balconies. 'did I really see that or was it my imagination' she thought to herself.

She moved the pictures back and forth. The image to her was real enough. But now, it was gone. She paused for a moment, wondering if she was just imagining the vision. The stress she had been going through, taking its toll. She shrugged the thoughts out of her mind and continued. The more she looked, the more she was convinced that the choice made, was the best one.

Kevin returned to the dining room with a cup of coffee and placed it on the table.

"what do you think?" he asked.

"looks really nice. I hope the owner gets back to us soon."

A message bubble appeared in the corner of the screen. It was a notification about an email. Clara stood up from her seat, side stepped and allowed Kevin to sit down.

He waved the cursor to the bubble and clicked. The screen momentarily went white and then revealed the email.

"it's from the Megali Luxuries." He replied.

Clara leaned over Kevin's shoulder and started to read.

"this is great news!"

"looks like we are going away on holiday!" he replied, the excitement hardly contained.

Clara walked through to the kitchen, whistling Zorba the Greek. It was time to start preparing the dinner and she did with an energetic zest and spring in her step. For the first time in weeks, she was starting to feel positive, not just in herself but for her family and the future.

She didn't realise that, first they would have to go through hell before they got there.

Kevin remained at the laptop. He replied to the email and had now started to look for the flights they needed.

After an hour, he entered the kitchen. Walked up to Clara and wrapped his arms around her. She felt a warmth envelope her as he did.

"the flights and apartment are booked. We will be going in just over a weeks' time."

Clara clapped her hands together. "excellent" she replied and proceeded to hum Zorba the Greek again. This time, Kevin joined in. The volume grew. Kevin's humming turned into imitating a guitar and he started dancing around the kitchen. Clara found this amusing. Watching her husband pretending that he is a Greek dancer.

"all we need is the plate smashing now! Can we break a few?" came a voice from the kitchen doorway. It was William. Unheard by Kevin and Clara, he had come downstairs and watched the display without saying a word. Kevin was crouching down to the floor. Williams voice making him jump into the air in surprise and the fun ceased.

"blimey bud, I didn't see you there!". He turned to see Clara laughing. "what's happening?" William asked.

Clara walked over to William and took hold of his hands. "we have the holiday all booked. We are going to Corfu." She replied.

William thrust himself into Clara's arms and started hugging her.

"thank you, mum, dad."

Chapter 6.

The days passed slowly. Kevin, Clara and the children spent the following week, going about their daily routines. Clara had only one bad dream. It, as with the others was powerful enough to wake her in the early hours of the morning. She had dreamt, as before, Of the park. William going missing and her frantic search for him. Everything was almost the same as before. She had made it to the clearing and could see the rocks. William, again as before. Was standing at the top. A black line started appeared to be coming out of the rocks. It split into two. One line carried on, as in her dreams before. The other, directly towards her. Fear took hold. She turned to look at the treeline. Kevin and Charlotte were not there as before. Noticing the line of crickets gaining ground on her. She turned and threw her body into a full sprint to the trees.

Her feet catching and stumbling in the uneven ground. Nothing was going to stop her. She was nearing the area where Kevin and Charlotte had been standing before. Turning her head, she noticed that the crickets were still coming. They hadn't gained ground on her and yet, although she had been running as fast as she could, she was no further away from them. Her strides were long and yet she was no further away from them, with their small legs.

Clara didn't want to see anymore. She wanted out of this nightmare. She felt that she had part control over it. As she approached the treeline, the sound of the crickets was horrendous. Ringing through her mind. She took one last look. They were still coming. The line reaching all the way back to the rocks. She could see the rocks, but William had gone. This was different to before. In all the dreams she had had, William had always been there. Now this turn of events was scaring the life out of her. She jumped over a small ditch lined with nettles. She hoped this would stop them, but as she got a few strides away from it, she turned to look again.

It was almost as if the ditch was not there. They merely jumped over and continued towards her. As she turned to face the front, she could see a tree branch and totally misjudged the height of it. Seconds later, it made contact, with her face. Small twigs from the branch slammed into her cheeks. She winced in pain as a couple pierced into her skin. It made her reel backwards. Her feet no longer had a grip on the ground, and she fell backwards. As she fell, she could see the branches waving to her in the breeze. Then the sky appeared. She could hear the crickets chirping in approval, as if to celebrate the fact that the tree had felled their enemy. Then darkness filled her vision, and she awoke.

For a moment, she could still hear the crickets, then silence.

She laid for a few moments, then slowly drifted back to sleep.

The morning came and she woke as normal, got dressed and went downstairs to prepare breakfast.

Kevin and the children were already there. Kevin was in the kitchen helping by getting bowls out of the cupboard and lining up the different cereals. The kettle had boiled just as Clara arrived. After making two teas, she sat down quietly, with a bowl of cereal and she ate in silence. Kevin knew something was wrong but didn't want to say anything in front of the children. he would wait until they had left the room to talk to her about what she had dreamt.

The children left the kitchen, Charlotte returned upstairs to get ready for school and William got changed and switched on his games console. Today was they day of his tests. He wasn't too sure what he was expected to do. So being slightly confused he decided to play games until it was time to go.

Kevin sat down next to Clara. "are you ok? You seem very quiet this morning." He asked.

"I had another dream last night. It was worse than before" she replied.

"oh."

"I'm worried" and she explained.

"I don't think it's anything to worry about. Your just stressed."

"but it is scaring me. I'm worried that it has something to do with William."

"William will be fine. We will get these tests out the way and enjoy the holiday. Let's just wait and see." Kevin replied sympathetically.

Clara picked up her cup and walked towards the kitchen. "you think it's because I'm stressed?"

Kevin followed behind. "I think you are not just stressed, your worried about William as well. He's going to go through some horrible things over the next week and we have to be there to support him."

Clara agreed and headed upstairs to get changed.

She passed Charlotte on the stairs. "I'm off to school now mum."

"ok honey." And she gave Charlotte a peck on the cheek and walked up to the bathroom. Moments later, she could hear the door shut, as Charlotte walked to the bus stop. She placed her various items of make up along the windowsill, in front of the mirror. She still wanted to look her best, even if it was the hospital. Picking up the hairbrush and stroking it through her hair, she began whistling Zorba the Greek again. It made her happy, as it was bringing happy thoughts to her of the holiday. She wanted the family to enjoy the time they will have together. She was picturing the beach and the pool as her hair started to become straighter. Over her whistling, she heard a familiar and haunting noise.

The sounds of the crickets had returned again. She threw the hairbrush into the sink and looked directly at her reflection in the mirror. On her right shoulder, sat a jet-black cricket. its rear legs, rubbing together, creating the sound that Clara had now grown to hate. Its black eyes blending in with the rest of its body. There was something in those eyes that alarmed her even more. In the centre of each eye, was a circle of oddly coloured light. She couldn't quite make out what it was, but it looked familiar.

"what the hell!" she called out. And she tried to focus on the image. The sound stopped and she noticed that the cricket's legs had stopped rubbing also. They were tucked up alongside its body. Suddenly it pounced. It threw itself directly at the mirror. As it got closer, its eyes became larger. Clara could see what the image was, in its eyes. It was William. His face slightly contorted.

Williams face was the last thing she saw before she fainted and fell in a heap on the floor.

In the darkness, she could hear Williams voice "mummy, mummy."

She turned her head to look around. Clara was alone in the darkness, but Williams voice could still be heard. Finding that she was able to move, she sat up. Clara closed her eyes, hoping that, when she opened them again, she would be back in the bathroom once more. Slowly, she found the courage and opened them. Her surroundings were still in pitch black. To her right she noticed a small light. She got to her feet and started to walk towards it. Williams voice, still called out to her, but now she could hear a faint quiver in his voice. It was coming from the source of the light.

Her pace picked up and she began to run. The light grew larger, Williams voice got louder.

As she got closer, Clara could see, she was in a tunnel. The light was bouncing of the sides and illuminating the exit. Her eyes started to adjust as the light got brighter. She could make out the different colours. Long, green Grass on the ground, the bright blue sky and a pile of grey rocks. She had to blink and shake her head in disbelief. It was the pile of rocks from her dream. She cleared the entrance to the tunnel and headed towards them. She could feel the heat from the sun as before in her dreams. "William!" she shouted. "mummy! Mummy!" came the reply and in an instant, Clara could see him standing on the rocks.

This time, Clara had had enough of these dreams and visions. She started to run again. Directly towards the pile of rocks and William. This time she didn't care. She was angry and had enough.

She didn't like crickets, but she wouldn't stand to see her son like this in the visions anymore. Before she could reach the rocks, the crickets began to crawl out of a small crevice at the base. Horrible, black and crawling. Looking in all directions. As soon as they saw Clara, they split into two columns. One line towards William, the other, towards her. As they approached, Clara began to stomp down onto the floor. They weren't going to get her or William. She managed to kill a few. Then they seemed to get a collective thought and simultaneously started to dodge every incoming foot. Looking up at her in annoyance. They still hadn't got to William. She pushed forward. A few had managed to jump onto her leg. She shrieked and brushed at them with her hands. Little black bodies flew in all directions as she ran. Eventually she reached the rocks and began to scramble up the side.

"Mummy! You are here! You come to get me!" he cried.

"yes sweety! I'm here!"

More and more of the crickets poured out. The more she killed or brushed away, the more they came. Clara was determined to get William and get away from this nightmare. She reached William before them. Swept him up in her arms, just as the first line of the bugs reached where his feet were.

"I'm taking you home!" she said and almost jumped off the top of the rocks. With two steps she was back onto the grass and sprinting away.

The action took the crickets off guard and a gap had opened between them. With a clear lead, Clara was hopeful that they would get away.

Clara was getting tired. William wasn't easy to carry and it was getting harder to run. She was getting tired. She looked about for the tunnel entrance that she had run out of earlier, but it was nowhere to be seen. She could see the treeline at the edge of the field. Still no tunnel.

Her pace slowed and she took a quick glance behind her. The crickets had slowed down. they were still advancing towards them, but the gap was increasing.

She suddenly remembered the ditch and the branch that hit her in the previous dream. Without thinking, she leapt over the ditch and immediately turned to the left to avoid the branch. Tiredness now ripped through her body and her legs began to ache. "I'm sorry William, I need to put you down. you will have to run as fast as you can" she whispered into his ear, as she lowered him down.

William had been watching the crickets following them from the rocks. "it's ok mummy. They have stopped following us and they are going back to the rocks. Look!" He replied. Clara stopped. Turned around and looked. They had near enough gone. A few straggling crickets were still making their way back. They were stopping at the corpses of their fallen comrades. Eventually they disappeared. Nothing remained in the field now, apart from the dead.

Clara now felt safe. She had won, but for how long.

As she cleared the branches of the trees, she came to another clearing. Another field. Exactly the same as the one William was in. only instead of a pile of rocks, a tunnel entrance stood in its place. A dark circular tube, rose out of the ground, aiming towards the sky. The two of them started walking towards it. The only thing worrying Clara was, will the crickets be down there? When she woke in the darkness previously, there were none. However. She couldn't remember passing through the treeline when she exited the tunnel and headed towards William. It was a risk she was going to have to take. The tunnel it was going to have to be.

Cautiously, they approached. Watching in all directions, in case the crickets appeared. Clara leant on the side and leaned her head into the entrance. She took a deep breath and focused her concentration on hearing for anything inside.

There was nothing but a distant dripping from deep inside. The echo of every droplet cascade through. If this was where she entered, then this must be the way out and they started to walk into the tunnel.

William was scared. A few years ago, he had grown out of his fear of the dark. Now it returned. Even Clara was scared. They were descending into a dark abyss, not knowing what was down there. Were the crickets waiting for them or was this the way to their salvation and freedom.

The light grew dimmer behind them. It started to become difficult to see. Even when Clara turned and looked down at William, she struggled to see his silhouette against the fading light. After a few minutes walking, they were in total darkness. Even the tunnel entrance had now gone. A mere pinprick of light was barely visible. But that wasn't her concern. All she wanted to do was get home. She wanted Kevin. For some reason, unlike the previous times. Even Kevin and Charlotte had been present, but not now. They were alone.

Clara had no idea how far down they needed to go. She hadn't counted steps or timed herself when she left the other tunnel. She realised it would just be a case of continuing to walk until something happens or they couldn't go any further. Without warning Clara tripped and she lunged forward. Her hand let go of William. Stumbling in the darkness she screamed out to him as her body plummeted to the ground.

"William!"

"Mummy! Mummy!"

She could hear him, but not see him. She began groping around in the dark, hoping her hands would contact her sons.

She feared, she was going to be left on her own again. William too, was frantically trying to find his mother in the darkness. Reaching out in all directions.

"Mummy! Mummy!" he called again. His voice was loud and clear to Clara. Tears started to well in her eyes. She was scared she was going to lose him.

Again, she heard William call out. Only this time it was closer than before.

"mummy!"

"mummy!"

"MUMMY!"

Suddenly, there was a flash of brilliant white light and Clara was back in the bathroom, laying on the floor. William was crouched down beside her, holding her hand.

"mummy! Are you ok?" he pleaded.

Clara blinked a few times and coughed. Nodding her head, she looked directly at William. She raised her hand and gently stroked his face.

"yes honey. I'm fine" she replied and sat up to gain her composure. A few minutes later, she was back up and standing in front of the mirror, adjusting her makeup. Soon she would be ready for the day. But it would not stop the memories of the bathroom.

By the time Clara got downstairs, Kevin had left for work. He had an important meeting with his employers. As she walked into the kitchen, Clara could see a piece of paper on the table. It was a note from Kevin.

She picked it up.

'honey

I have gone into work. Please keep me updated on the tests today.

Love you all.

Kevin xx'

She placed the note to her chest. She felt so lucky, to have such a loving husband and wonderful children.

William came walking into the kitchen. "are you ok now mum?" he asked.

"yes sweety. I just had a little scare that's all."

William approached her and put his arms around her. "are we going to the hospital soon mummy?"

"yes. If you go and put your trainers on and we will go."

William ran down the hallway to the shoe rack and sat down on the floor. He picked up his trainers and untied the laces. He had only just started to learn to tie them. For weeks he would end up just tying the laces into various knots, despite Kevin, Clara and Charlotte spending, hour after hour, showing him. He started to struggle. Clara walked down to him and knelt down. she then proceeded to talk him through, tying his laces.

"the rabbit went over the hill and down the hole. Later he came back out again" and she pulled the two laces. She made a rabbit ear with one of them.

"the rabbit jumped into the air and back down. Then another rabbit came a long and they began to play" and she looped one around the other and poked it through to make the second rabbit ear. Clara had started to double tie the rabbit ears. William was so energetic, running around and playing games in the garden. The laces would always untie themselves.

William jumped up off the floor and bounded in towards the kitchen.

Clara looked at her watch. They had half an hour before they needed to be at the hospital. So, she decided that she would just sit in the kitchen and watch William play in the garden, finish her tea and then head off.

She sat calmly and started looking in her to do list for their holiday. Everything was ready. They had their currency. All passports were in date and all bags were packed. Everything was relying on today's tests. If the procedures went without a hitch, they would be on their way to Corfu in two days' time.

Chapter 7.

The sun was beating down after a small shower, as they pulled into the car park of the hospital. Clara took the ticket out of the machine and began looking for a space. Fortunately, it didn't take long to find one. She pulled in and killed the engine. The traffic had been moderate, and the journey was quick. Clara looked at her watch. They still had twenty minutes before the appointment. They both got out of the car and started to walk towards the hospital entrance. The footpath seemed to be a mile long. It winded to the left and right. Meandering through willow tree saplings that had been planted the year before.

William was thrilled by the scene. To each side of the path, beyond the willows, were large ponds. Ducks splashed and bathed. Here and there were seagulls strolling by, looking for scraps of food that anyone had thrown down for the birds. Every now and then, they could hear a splashing sound. When they looked, they could see ripples in the water.

"what was that mum?" William asked.

Clara wasn't too sure. "I think they have put fish into the ponds William." He was fascinated and wanted to stop. Clara was only interested in getting to the reception and letting them know they were there. She gently tugged his arm. "please William, we need to get to the doctor!"

Hearing her plea. He started to walk. "Can we watch for the fish when we come out please?" Clara agreed. "maybe we can get something to eat and sit out here on the benches" William loved his idea and began to skip with excitement. Moments later, they arrived in the reception of the paediatric department.

It was the same lady on the reception as before, when it was just Clara and Kevin. She recognised Clara immediately. She stopped what she was doing and stood up from behind the counter to greet them.

"hello Mrs Dwyer. I take it, this is little William?"

Clara by now was a little nervous and just gave a smile and nodded her head.

"hello" William replied smiling.

Clara found the courage to reply "ah, yes. We are here for the appointment with Doctor Parker."

The receptionist sat back down and typed into the computer. "lovely! That's fine. Please take a seat."

Clara turned and looked at the seats. She didn't want to seat where she had before. After the moment in the bathroom and the previous experience there. She was determined that no more today, was she going to see those horrible things. In the far corner of the waiting area, were some seats facing a large tv screen. The tv was on. The volume was down low. Running across the bottom were the subtitles. Clara wasn't too bothered. It was a gardening show. William would be ok with that and as long as she didn't have to stare out of that window again, she would be happy. They sat down and immediately; William was engrossed with the tv.

He was transfixed. The man on the show was planting different varieties of summer and autumn blooming flowers. He was describing each one as he was planning them.

"Mummy. Can we have some of those for our garden?" and he pointed at the television.

The presenter had been describing the different types of lilies and what time of year they needed to be planted and when they bloom.

Clara smiled "what ones would you like to have?"

William looked at the screen. "I like them one's mummy! Can we have those?"

Clara looked up and saw a beautiful green stem of colour, with large orange trumpets.

"they look lovely William" she replied. "when we get back from our holiday, we will go and look for some." As she looked again the name came across the screen. Quickly, Clara withdrew her phone from her handbag and opened the menu. Opened the notes and wrote 'African Queen lilies.'

She placed the phone back into her bag and looked around the waiting room. She could see the receptionist walking towards them.

Her heart jumped into her throat. The nerves were finally kicking in. she wasn't spending too much time thinking about what was going to happen. She had been trying to block it all out of her mind.

The receptionist knelt down in front of them. "the Doctor is ready for you now" she said softly.

They got up and turned away from the television and took Williams hand and began to walk towards the Doctors office.

William didn't seem to be bothered about the tests. Bot Kevin and Clara both agreed that they didn't think he even knew what danger this virus could bring. He just skipped along the corridor. "mummy, as we have a big enough garden. Could we just get different types of lilies?"

"I don't see why not."

"yay!" William called out. His voice echoing down the corridor.

She tapped on the door and pulled down on the handle. At exactly the same time, the Doctor was also pulling down on the handle and the door swung open. Clara staggered forward, looked up at Doctor Parker. They both laughed as Clara and William entered the room.

The Doctor sat down. "and how are you both feeling today?"

"we are good thank you" Clara replied.

"and you William?"

"I'm good thank you" he shyly replied. And he tucked himself up into Clara's side.

"wonderful. So, today we will do a very small biopsy and a blood test. We have a private room for the both of you. Once the tests are done you will be able to go home again."

"great! Do you know when that will be? So, I can keep my husband up to date" Clara asked.

He rifled through his notes. "hopefully, we should be able to let you go before five this evening. The tests themselves, won't take long. But we need to make sure everything is ok with William first. The results of the bloods will come back pretty quick. The biopsy results will take a day or two. So, providing William feels ok to go home later, then all would be good for you both to leave."

Clara was pleased to hear this. She didn't want to be there any longer than they needed to be and with the Doctors assurance, felt comforted.

Doctor Parker rose from his desk and picked up his paperwork.

"ok. Let's get you two to your room, shall we?" and he motioned them to the door. Clara and William got up. Clara picked up her bag and they walked towards the door. There was very little talk on the way. William would just stare out of the windows as they walked down the corridors towards the children's ward. Clara and the Doctor didn't say a word.

The sign for paediatrics came into sight. William saw it before Clara.

"what does that word say mummy?" he asked.

Clara found it amusing. She found the word difficult to say herself for many years and would pronounce it wrong. "it basically says children's ward."

"oh. We are here then?"

"yes, and we have our own room."

"cool" and he began skipping again, as the approached the department door. Doctor Parker opened the door and directed them through into the ward.

"we just have to sign you in" and he walked into the office. Moments later he returned with a nurse and they followed them into a side ward full of individual rooms. They entered the first room and Clara placed her bag onto a chair by the side of the bed.

"here we are young sir" the nurse laughed.

William found it funny and jumped onto the bed. He leaned over to the remote sitting on the wall and began pressing the buttons. The bed started to lift up. Doctor Parker spotted the fun William was having "right little rollercoaster ride you have their William" and he laughed.

He tried different buttons that made either end go up and down. Clara was getting a little annoyed and demanded him to stop. Straight faced, he put the remote down on the side table and crossed his arms.

"oh dear." Said the nurse.

This seemed to make William cross, and he sat back against the wall.

The Doctor placed the notes into a tray. "ok we will be back in about half an hour, to start the preparations for the biopsy." With that, they walked out of the room, leaving Clara and William alone.

Above him was a small tv screen connected to a metal arm. She pulled it down and pressed the power button on the side. It lit up like a Christmas tree. Colours flashed across the screen to reveal the hospital trusts logo. Then a menu appeared of the different channels that were available.

Clara picked up the remote control and pressed the direction buttons. She selected a cartoon channel, altered the volume and placed the remote back onto the table. William instantly started to laugh. It was Tom and Jerry and as always, poor Jerry was yet again being chased.

Time went quickly and before they knew it, Doctor parker knocked on the door and let himself in. "the nurse will be here in a moment to get William ready. Would it be possible for William to take his jacket off?"

Clara walked over to William.

She instructed him to remove his jacket, which he did quickly.

The nurse arrived with a small wheelchair.

She had a huge smile on her face. "your taxi awaits sir."

William jumped off the bed and threw himself into the chair. "I would like to go to London please" and he laughed. "no problem guvnor!" she replied, spinning the chair round to face the door.

The nurse opened the door and pushed with force. Williams feet lifted into the air. "yahoo!" he shouted as he went racing down the corridor. Clara and the Doctor followed behind. They turned and went through another set of doors into a small operating room.

In the centre of the room was a large chair, similar to that of a dentist's chair. To the side was a table with trays full of varying instruments, neatly laid on paper towels. Clara winced when she saw a barbaric looking drill.

Doctor Parker approached Clara, "ok Mrs Dwyer. If you wouldn't mind leaving the operating room. We will begin the procedure in a few minutes."

"you can wait in the room and we will bring William back as soon as we are done" the nurse added.

"ok" she replied. She walked over to William and leant towards him.

"see you in a minute honey" and gave him a kiss on the forehead, stroked his cheek and walked out of the room. A tear welling in her eyes. She didn't like the thought of what they were going to do. But she knew that it was his life at stake. She walked into the room and picked up her handbag. She decided to go outside for some air and see if she could talk to Kevin. She didn't really like the clinical smell of hospitals. They smelt too clean. As soon as she reached the outer doors of the reception. The sliding doors parted, and the familiar smells of the outside rushed her nostrils. She breathed a sigh of relief and walked towards the benches by one of the ponds.

A fragrant breeze blew towards her from the other side of the pond. As it travelled, ripples swept from one side to the other. Clara watched amused, as the ducks bobbed their heads under the water to catch loose weeds stirred up by the motion. She sat down and opened her phone. Dialled Kevin's number and waited for him to pick up.

"hiya" came Kevin's voice from the other end. "you have caught me just in time. I'm about to go into the meeting. Is everything ok?"

"yes. Thought I would call to say, he has just gone into the operating room. They reckon he will be out in about half an hour." She replied.

"ok. My meeting should only take about an hour. Would you like me to come to the hospital after? The boss says I can go home after."

"William would love that."

"ok. I will be there as quick as I can. See you later" and the phone went dead.

Clara didn't get the chance to reply. She just looked at the phone to see the call had ended.

Inside the operating room, William sat calmly as the Doctor and nurse where preparing. A theatre gown had been placed around his neck. William found it funny to move his hands from side to side, underneath.

"ok William. We will be starting now. Just something to numb the area where we are going to be working. Ok?"

"ok" he replied. His hands stopped moving and he became still.

Doctor Parker gently lifted up a small tuft of hair on the back of Williams head and the nurse placed a clip to hold it in place. It revealed a bare patch of skin for him to work on.

Feeling this happening, William closed his eyes. At the same time on the bench outside, Clara also closed her eyes and prayed for William to be ok.

What greeted Clara when her eyes closed, was not what she had expected. It was dark. But the familiar darkness of having her eyes closed during the daytime wasn't there. It was total darkness, almost pitch black.

"Mummy?" came a voice. It was William. He was beside her. she turned to face him but couldn't see how close he was. After a moment, her eyes adjusted and was able to make out his silhouette. He was close but just out of reach. She shuffled slightly and held out her hand.

"it's ok honey I'm here!" she called. Williams hand contacted with hers. She grasped it and pulled him closer. He wrapped his arms round her.

"where are we mum? I'm scared."

"I'm not sure sweety. But I'm here and I won't let anything hurt you. Ok?"

"yes mummy." And he squeezed a little tighter.

Clara felt something on her nose. she wiped it with her hand and sniffed. She smelt something familiar and wondered where she had smelt it before. It took a moment, then she realised. It was the tunnel from her dream. They were back. But how?

She knew they were safe, but for how long? But she knew they couldn't stay there, so she got up, whilst holding onto William. "we must leave here" and they started walking. There was no knowing what was at the end of the tunnel at the entrance, but she would just have to take her chances and hope that the crickets were not waiting for them outside.

As they walked into the light, the familiar sights of the sky, the trees and the ground came into view. It was so bright, that they had to squint to be able to get the best view of their surroundings. There were no crickets. They had left the area and most likely back under the rocks.

Clara looked around. She wasn't sure where they were. This area was new to her, but they had to go somewhere. Somewhere safe and away from that pile of rocks.

She turned to face the tunnel. Behind the entrance, fifty feet away, Clara could see a fence running alongside the field. A line of trees lay beyond. She couldn't see anything passed them. As she watched, two small motorbikes whizzed past. The low buzzing noise evaporating into the distance as they got further away.

"we must get somewhere safe William" and they started walking towards the fence.

They walked past the tunnel entrance and headed across the field. William managed to find a few rabbit holes. Which, he promptly put his feet into, making him stumble. Clara would keep a hold of him and managed to stop him going face first into the ground. She as determined to protect him.

On the other side of the field, in the treeline. Sat a lone cricket. high up in the branches, it sat silently. Watching every movement Clara and William made. Its antennae waving back and forth. The crickets were now displaying a form of intelligence. They wouldn't use their legs to communicate. The waving of the antennae was being used as semaphore. In the field on the other side of the treeline. In a line, were more crickets doing the same. Sitting silently waving the same message to each other, one at a time, passing the message down the line, until it had reached the base of the rock pile.

Clara and William had now reached the fence. The wire connected to each post sagging towards the ground. She looked along the fence, to see if there was a place that they would be able to climb over without snagging themselves on the barbs. A few sections down, a section had hardly any cable. Clara hoisted William over, then joined him on the other side of the fence. Now they were standing on a small dirt track road.

Clara had now got to decide which direction there were going to go.

Chapter 8.

Her decision was made quickly. As she was watching the road. The sounds of the crickets returned. Fear now rose and Clara began to panic. Her breathing laboured from the walk across the field.

William felt nothing of what the Doctor was doing. He couldn't feel the scalpel piercing his skin and making a two-centimetre-long incision across the back of his head. He passed the scalpel back to the nurse, who then handed a small drill. Still motionless, William could feel the pressure as the Doctor pressed the drill into his skull. Then a high-pitched whirring noise, as he pressed the button to start drilling. The sound echoed throughout the room.

William could hear something else. His mind was in two places. He could hear Clara speaking to him. But there was something else. Under her voice, he could hear crickets chirping. Various tones, as if a group of them were talking to each other. He closed his eyes, and he was no longer there. He was standing on a dirt tracked road with Clara and holding her hand, they were walking down the road.

"mummy, where are we going?" he asked.

"trying to get out of here."

"where too?"

Clara wasn't too sure where, but as long as they were away from the fields and that pile of rocks. She didn't really care. The track arched to the right and she could see farm sheds, then buildings. She looked behind them. Nothing and no one were following them. She couldn't see any crickets or hear them either. She took a deep breath to calm herself down. in front of them, the track seemed to be endless. The horizon miles away. She hoped that soon they would reach the end and there would be some way of getting out of this.

As they walked, William placed his hand on the back of his head.

Clara stopped and knelt down. "are you ok honey."

"yes mummy. I'm ok. Just a little headache" he replied and the continued walking. Clara could only assume that the situation and the sun had contributed to his headache.

Neither of them knew that the crickets had followed them. They were still watching from a distance and talking to each other without Clara and William seeing them. They were unaware of what was happening behind them. They had massed together; a collective had gathered a short distance away.

Villas and houses passed them as they made their way into a lightly built-up area. Clara stopped dead in here tracks. Staring, wide eyed. Dead ahead was a taverna. They were in Greece. The lettering on the building was bold and recognisable. She couldn't understand why they were there, as much as she couldn't understand the rest of what was happening to them both. One thing was missing. A taverna with no people. The only people she thought she saw, were the people on the motorbikes when they were standing in the field. She tried to picture what she saw. Thinking back at the field, she never actually saw the people on them. Their bodies seemed to be blurred as the rode by.

The panic started to return. There were no people around, anywhere. Eventually, they came to the end of the road. They were standing in front of the bluest sea and a sandy beach. A tarmacked road spread from left to right. in each direction Clara looked, there were no people. Shops, restaurants and taverna's were everywhere, but they were all empty.

They crossed over the road to try and get a better look. William tugged on Clara's hand. "mummy! They are coming!" he shouted in fear. His voice trembling.

They turned to face where they had walked from, the sun directly in their faces.

Clara gasped as her eyes began to focus down the road. In the distance, she could see a large black mass moving down the road. With the mass came a faint droning sound and as the line came closer, the sound grew louder. William tightened his grip. "it's the crickets mummy!"

"no!" she shouted and turned to look, to see what direction they should go.

There were no people to help them and nowhere they could go to get themselves out the way.

She tugged Williams hand hard and they started to run along the road.

But the crickets still advanced. Clara turned to look. The crickets had reached the end of the road and were starting to walk their way. Clara now had to think quickly. She looked at the water. 'can crickets swim?' she thought. There was only one way to find out. She jumped down onto the sand and held her arms out. William jumped off and into her arms, swinging them around to face the sea. "we need to stop them William. I don't think they will follow us into the water" she whispered into his ear.

She put him down. with a few steps, water had filled their shoes as they walked into the sea. Clara looked behind. They were standing on the edge of the road. None of them went onto the sand or tried to go into the water after them. They took a few more steps until the sea reached Williams waist. They could see them sitting there watching them.

Crude looking beasts, their antennae swaying from side to side. The chirping sound from their legs becoming almost unbearable. The more that joined the mass, the louder the sound became.

"how long do we have to stay here mummy?" William asked.

"hopefully, they will give up and go soon sweety" she replied. Truly, she had no idea. But found it comforting to say that to William and now the sun was starting to set. The colour of the sky, changing from blue to a light orange, to dark orange and red.

It started to get colder as the sun dipped below the horizon and a chill came in with the current of the sea.

The sea wall where the crickets were sitting in wait, became harder to see. The chirping being almost the only way of knowing if they were still there. The streets were still empty and were void of people and vehicles, but some lights were on, casting a few beams of light along the road.

Clara shivered and looked at William. She knew he must be getting as cold as she was.

"are you ok?" as she stroked his head.

"yes mummy! My headache has gone" he replied.

As he said that the daylight extinguished, and the night started to take hold. They could no longer see the road or the edge of the beach. Clara hadn't noticed that the crickets had gone. The chirping had ceased.

Without warning the lights on the streets and buildings went out and they were now not only cold and wet, but in total darkness. The only thing they could hear, was the sound of the waves lapping against the beach. Eventually, even that sound began to fade. "we will be ok William. We will go back to the road in a minute" she whispered.

William looked at her "its ok mummy, we can go back now" and suddenly there was a bright flash of brilliant white light and Clara was sitting back on the bench in front of the pond. The gentle breeze, still blowing. She looked at her watch. Half an hour had passed, which now confused her. They must have been in this nightmare for at least a few hours. Clara wasn't sure how this happened. But her concern now was for William.

She stood up, picked up her bag and made her way back to the children's ward. She was certain that William would be out of the operating theatre by now. She decided to stop at the shop and buy a few snacks for herself and William. Minutes later, she was sitting in the cosy armchair next to Williams bed.

She knew they wouldn't be much longer, so she switched the television on and sat watching cartoons. Her phone vibrated. It was Kevin. She picked up the phone and answered. "hi honey."

"hiya. I'm just coming int the car park now. So, I should be with you in a few minutes. Has William come out yet?"

Clara was going to keep tight lipped about what she experienced earlier. She wasn't going to cause more alarm. "no not yet. I went outside for a while. I've just got back to the room. He shouldn't be much longer."

"that's good. I'd like to be there when he comes back in." he replied.

Clara realised she was thirsty, so now she would take the opportunity to ask. "can you get a coffee on the way up?" she asked.

"of course. I will be there in a mo." And he cancelled the call.

She was happy that Kevin had managed to get back in time. He and William were inseparable. They spent a lot of time together when Kevin wasn't working. Playing games or football in the back garden. He did also spend time with Charlotte, but as she was older and more independent. The only thing she would do with her parents was shopping. The rest of her time was devoted to her friends.

There was a knock at the door and Clara rose to answer it. She opened the door and there was Kevin. A bag full of various foods, hanging from his elbow and a cup of coffee in each hand. He tried to mumble something but the packet of custard creams hanging from his mouth, restricted his ability to speak.

Laughing, Clara opened the door fully to allow her heavily ladened husband through.

He placed the cups down on the table. Spat the biscuits onto the bed and threw the bag down beside them. He turned and put his arms around Clara and gave her a hug and that was how they stayed for a few minutes. Until Kevin remembered that the coffee was going cold.

They sat down and continued to wait.

They could both here Williams voice coming from the corridor. He was laughing and joking with Doctor Parker and the nurse. Then the room door opened, and they came rushing into the room.

"Daddy!" William shouted. Kevin jumped out of his chair and gave William a hug.

"hiya, buddy!" he replied.

Clara rose from the bed where she had been sitting, walked over and crouched by the side of William and Kevin.

"how do you feel?" she asked. She was wondering if he had the same experience as she did. She wouldn't ask about it in front of the Doctor and the nurse. She would wait until Kevin and herself were alone to talk to him about it. She didn't want to scare the children unnecessarily.

"I'm fine mummy" William laughed back.

She rose and approached the Doctor.

"how did it go?"

"it went better than we expected. William was amazing. He remained calm throughout the procedure."

"excellent" and she turned to face William. "and what about scarring?" She didn't like the thought that her son may have a scar for life, even though Doctor Parker had assured them there wouldn't be.

"that is fine. Where we needed to take the biopsy from, we had a nice large tuft of hair that covers the area. So, there will be no visible scar."

Kevin released his grip from around William and walked over to join the conversation.

"when will the results be returned?"

"they should take between one to two weeks. As soon as they arrive at my office, I will contact you immediately."

Kevin nodded his approval.

Clara looked at Kevin, then back to the doctor. "we are going away in a few days' time, for a couple of weeks, for a holiday. Is that ok?" she asked.

Doctor Parker placed his right hand in his coat pocket and retrieved a small package. "that is perfect. After the time you guys have had recently. You deserve the rest. All I ask you to do is, about this time tomorrow, take off the current dressing and replace it with this one. After a couple of days, it should be fine to remove and leave it off."

"wonderful." She replied.

"are you going anywhere nice" asked the nurse.

"I hope so." Kevin replied. "we are heading to Corfu."

"wow! A lovely place. Have you been before?"

"no. this will be the first time. I have been to the Greek mainland before but not there" Clara added.

The nurse walked over to William and stroked his shoulder. "well, I hope you guys have a fabulous time" and with that, she walked out of the room.

Doctor Parker handed the dressing pack to Clara. "I must be going now; I have another appointment to attend. As soon as the blood results are back, I will return with the notes and hopefully the discharge papers."

He shook Kevin's hand and left, leaving them alone.

"is Charlotte ok?" Kevin asked.

"yes. She was a little worried about today, but she is ok. She is going to her friend Sarah's after school. We have to give her a call when we are home and Sarah's dad will bring her back."

Kevin was now wheeling William over to the bed. "cool. Maybe if we leave here at the right time, we can get some fried chicken on the way home."

"yummy!" William shouted, as he climbed up onto the oversized bed.

Within moments of William laying down, he was fast asleep.

Clara was glad. William had been through a fair bit that day and now he was sleeping, she would be able to speak to Kevin.

She took hold of the blanket and tucked him in. William stirred slightly, getting himself comfortable and then was still.

For a few minutes, there was silence. Clara finally found the courage to speak. "it happened again!"

"what happened? The dreams?"

"yes. Only this time, William was with me. We started in the tunnel. Found our way out and chased to some beach."

"you were chased? What by?" Kevin sounded rather alarmed by what Clara was revealing to him.

"the crickets again, thousands of them. We ended up in the water and had to wait until it got dark, to escape them."

"and William was with you all the time?"

"yes. He never left my side."

"when did this happen?"

"William was in the operating theatre, I was outside. Shortly after I called you. I sat on a bench, and I only closed my eyes for a minute and that was when it happened."

"what happened? The dream?"

"yes. They're all connected. Everyone that I have had, are all linked together. Each one I have seemed to progress from the previous one."

Kevin grabbed hold of Clara's hands. "was William in all of them?"

"yes. I wasn't too sure where we were. It wasn't until about the third one I had, when I discovered roughly where we were."

"where were you?"

"we were somewhere in Greece!"

Kevin's eyes opened in surprise. "Greece? What the hell!"

He sat down at the end of the bed. "not Corfu surely?"

"I don't know. The buildings had Greek writing on them. So, could be anywhere."

Kevin wasn't too happy about this latest piece of information.

"shall we change the holiday and go somewhere else?"

Clara looked a little confused. "I don't think there is any need to do that" she replied. Clara was still pointing her finger at stress being the cause.

"if you are sure about this. You seem to be describing these dreams as if you were there!"

"it's fine. We will still go!"

William slept for a couple of hours. Finally, he opened his eyes, outstretched his arms and yawned.

"mummy, daddy! I've just had the weirdest dream" he whispered.

Kevin and Clara both looked at each other.

Clara moved her chair closer to the bed and held Williams hand.

"really? What happened?" she asked.

William paused for a moment. "me and you were in some tunnel or something. We walked outside and it was really hot. We walked for ages and then these bugs started chasing us and we ended up walking into the sea."

Shocked at how descriptive William was, shocked both Clara and Kevin. He had had the same dream as Clara. What came next scared them even more, making Kevin start to question his sanity. He couldn't make sense of these experiences and put it down to something Clara and William would share only between themselves.

"that's the second time I have had the same dream!" he called out. A slight trembling in his voice.

"mummy, I'm scared!" and he began to cry.

Clara held William in her arms, allowing him to release countless amounts of glassy tears over her shoulder and down her back.

"it's ok honey. Everything will be fine."

Kevin walked over and held them both. He didn't understand what was happening. He just wanted it over. This nightmare was starting to affect them all. the only one so far, that wasn't in the equation was Charlotte. So far, she hadn't shown any signs of this ability to share dreams along with himself.

He waited a little until Williams crying became a gentle sobbing.

"when was the other time today that it happened?" he asked.

William raised his head. "it was when I was with the Doctor and nurse. They were doing something to my head. I closed my eyes, and I wasn't there anymore, I was in the tunnel with mummy!"

Clara gasped. She looked at Kevin. "that was when I was outside!"

Kevin nodded his head. "I think we need to talk about this. We go away in a couple of days' time. I don't want this to affect the holiday!"

Clara placed William back on the bed and swung the television round and pressed the button.

With the tv on, William instantly calmed down and he started giggling at the cartoons.

She rose from the chair and put her hand on Kevin's shoulder, looking at him sympathetically as she did.

"me and daddy are just going to pop out of the room for a minute ok sweety?"

"ok mummy" he replied.

Kevin stood up and walked over to him. "we shan't be long buddy."

"ok dad" and they walked out of the room.

Silently, they walked down through the ward and out into the main corridor. People were walking too and frow about their business. A few nurses were having a conversation outside the radiology department. The main reception came into view and as they walked in, Kevin side stepped and headed towards the small coffee shop.

"want one?"

But Clara didn't hear and carried on walking towards the exit.

"Clara!" he shouted. This snapped her out of it, and she stopped, looked and walked towards him.

"sorry. I was thinking about what happened."

"it's ok. I'm getting a coffee. Do you want one?" he asked dipping his hand into his pocket. the change rattling as his fingers twisted around a variety of coins.

"yes please. Think I need something to eat as well" and they walked inside the shop.

They stood in the queue, eying up the delicacies inside the display counter. Kevin already knew what he was going to have. Rows of sandwiches, biscuits and cakes sat begging at them to buy them. Clara knew Kevin would have already made his mind up. if they ever went into town and had coffee, he was always the same and brought the same thing. She was just as bad and tended to do the same. Although she would eye all the different things for sale, she would still go for the same item. She hoped that one day, she would break this habit and choose something else. Today wasn't going to be the day.

"can I help you" a voice called out.

Both Kevin and Clara looked up simultaneously. At the far end of the counter. Standing in the corner behind the till was a smallish man looking in their direction.

The words barista written on the left collar of his shirt.

Kevin found this amusing. "Christ. If this guy walked up this end, he wouldn't be able to see over the top of this counter look" and he discretely pointed in the barista's direction. Clara nudged him in the ribs.

"stop it!" she giggled.

"ah yes. Two lattes please" she replied.

"a millionaires shortbread a Bakewell tart please" Kevin added.

Clara faced Kevin and they both smiled and laughed at each other.

"thankyou" the barista replied.

Kevin and Clara almost jumped out of their skins, as a lady got up from behind the counter they were standing in front of.

"got it" she called out to the guy behind the till and she turned and proceeded to make the drinks. This made them laugh even more. Kevin began to get a stitch. He hadn't laughed like that in a while. After recent events, Clara was thinking the exact same thing.

After paying for their drinks, they walked out of the coffee shop and headed out towards the ponds.

They found the bench that Clara had sat on earlier and placed themselves comfortably in the seat. Placing their lattes down on the floor beside them and unwrapped their food. They wouldn't talk until they had finished their food.

Chapter 9.

Kevin ate his with a speed that Clara would never understand.

"how can you enjoy something, when it doesn't even touch the sides" she remarked.

Popping his fingertips into his mouth, one at a time and making pleasurable noises, he picked up his latte and laughed. "you know me and my shortbread babes. Can't resist it" and they laughed together.

Eventually, Clara finished hers and was sipping at her drink.

"I'm not sure what to make of all this."

"you're not?" Kevin replied. "you know more than me and I'm powerless to do anything about it!"

"William and I are linked in these dreams and I don't know how or why."

Kevin detected the fear in her voice.

"let's just see what happens over the next few days. The Doctor said the new blood results won't take long to come back. We can decide what to do later."

Clara wasn't sure if the holiday were a good idea, but if it were due to the stress, the holiday could probably be the best solution to the problem.

"I will have a chat with Doctor Parker when he returns."

"good idea. But I don't think you should mention the dreams too much. In a couple of days, we will all be by the pool, soaking in the sun and having fun." Kevin put his arm around Clara, and they sat watching the ducks swimming around the pond.

After a while, they finished their drinks and started to make their way back to William in his room.

Once inside, they sat and waited. Clara cuddled up with William watching the cartoons, while Kevin sat in the armchair and retrieved his emails. An hour passed. Charlotte had called Kevin and was chatting about William and what he had to endure in the operating theatre. She had a morbid fascination with medical procedures, and they all agreed that the way Charlotte was going, she would end up being a surgeon or vet.

She was glad that he was ok. She sounded excited when Kevin announced to her that they would be home soon.

She wanted to go to the hospital but was persuaded to stay with Sarah until they got home.

Eventually, the Doctor returned. Clipboard in his hands.

"hello. Is everyone ok?"

They all looked up. "yes. We are fine thanks" replied Kevin.

"good." And he walked over to the bedside.

"we have the results back on the blood work we did, and it confirms the virus is there."

Clara's heart sank. Kevin stood up "so what will that mean for William and what's next?"

The Doctor sighed. "we will have to wait for the results to come back on the biopsy. Once we they are in, we can determine what course of action to take next."

"how long will that be?" Clara asked. her voice whimpering. Her empathy towards William had grown at an astounding rate. She preferred it to be her that went through all of this, but there was nothing she could do about it.

The Doctor smiled. There is a slight backlog of tests to be done, but they have assured me, that it will take about a week and a half."

"we will still be away." Clara replied.

"that's ok, I can call you they day after you return. I wouldn't dream of disturbing you, especially if it was not so good news."

Kevin felt happy with the Doctors answer. "no problem Doctor. Thankyou."

"you're welcome. I will get the discharge papers arranged for you and then you can head off home." He started to walk over to William. He placed his hand on Williams head and gently removed the dressing. He smiled and placed it back down. "it's healing well. Good!" and he walked out of the room, heading towards the nurse's station to begin the paperwork.

William started to get dressed as the Doctor returned with the papers. He handed them to Clara, which she gratefully received and placed into her bag. "thank you, Doctor Parker."

"you are welcome!" he patted William on the shoulder and left.

William continued to get dressed. He slipped on his shoe's and attempted to lace up his trainers. Minutes later, he had finished. Laces tied perfectly. Clara spun round to face Kevin; her eyes were wide open." you see this?"

"oh my. Yes. How long have we been teaching him to do his laces?"

"absolute ages. But he just tied them without being prompted. This is amazing." But in Clara's mind, the question was bouncing around that the procedure and the business with the crickets may have something to do with it.

As they walked out of the ward, William insisted on saying goodbye to all the nurses and giving them a wave. They walked past the ponds and towards the carpark. William stopped by the ponds. He rested his hands on the back of a bench. Clara suddenly had a cold shiver run through her body. It was the same bench that she sat on earlier in the day.

Shrugging the feeling away, Clara tapped William on the back and tried to rush him away from the pond. "come along sweety. We need to get home."

"sorry mummy" he replied, and he began to skip along the footpath.

Clara took hold of Kevin's hand and gave him a loving smile. Once in the car, Kevin started the engine, and they were on their way home. Kevin couldn't wait to see the back of the hospital. He watched the hospital disappear in the rear-view mirror. The further away the got, the happier he became. For every mile they travelled, the closer they were to their holiday.

Kevin had received an email earlier in the day from the children's school. They were happy for the children to be absent for the two weeks because of Williams condition. Things for now were going their way, and he was glad of that. they pulled into their driveway. No sooner had the car stopped, when William had undone his seatbelt and was eagerly waiting with his hand on the door latch to get out.

"eager beaver!" Kevin called out. "you can't get into the house without the key!"

But it was too late. William had already got out of the car and was running towards the house. Kevin and Clara laughed and got out.

They were laughing all the way up the footpath to the front door. They could see William frantically trying to turn the handle to get in.

"steady on buddy. The door is locked" Kevin giggled.

William took a step back and looked at him. "oh!"

Kevin put the key in the lock and turned the key. William grabbed the handle, shoved the door and shot into the hallway and rushed up the stairs. "Charlotte! Charlotte!" he shouted. Then it went silent.

"do you think he has just realised Charlotte isn't here?" and he came plodding down the stairs with a look of disappointment on his face.

"where is Charlie?"

Clara was putting her coat in the cupboard. "she will be back soon honey!"

Kevin was in the kitchen talking to Sarah's parents on the phone. William walked in, just as Kevin cancelled the call and put his phone down on the counter.

"is she coming home soon, I can't wait to see her and tell what happened!"

Kevin put his hands on his shoulders, "Sarah's dad is bringing her home in a minute. They are just finishing their dinner and they she will be back."

"ok" and he ran back upstairs into his bedroom.

Half an hour passed, and a car pulled up outside the house. Kevin heard a door slam, the car pulled away, the horn beeping as it went. Then the front door opened. Charlotte had returned. Within seconds, they heard William's door fly open, banging on the inside of his bedroom wall. He came full sprint down the stairs and rushed Charlotte. She hadn't even had the time to put her school bag down and remove her coat. She saw him just in time and she opened her arms. William ran into her and gave her a hug.

"sis! You won't believe this. I went to hospital and they drilled a hole into the back of my head. It was really weird, and I was awake the whole time."

Charlotte didn't know what to say. She just looked down at him, raised her eyebrows. "cool" and dropped her bag to the floor. She was pleased to see him. She just didn't expect him to have so much energy after being at the hospital all day. He had more than he did in the morning when she left.

As she took her coat off, she began to ask the questions that had taken her all day to think up.

"did you lose loads of blood?"

She knew he would exaggerate his answers but would humour him anyway.

"oh yeah! I lost loads. It was dripping down my head and onto the floor. They had to mop it all up, put it back into syringes, and inject it back into my head. But it kept on coming back out. It was well gory."

This explanation of events had them both in hysterics and they walked into the kitchen clutching their sides, they were laughing so hard.

Clara was reading through a takeaway menu as they entered.

"evening Charlotte. Did you have fun at your friends?"

Charlottes laughing calmed a little "yes mum, thanks."

"good. Are you hungry? We are getting a takeaway tonight. Do you want some?"

Charlotte pondered the question for a little. "yes please. Sarah's mum did fajitas. I don't really like them. I ate one, then couldn't eat anymore."

Clara knew that Charlotte wasn't too keen on spicy foods and She wasn't impressed. When Charlotte and William had friends over. They always asked in advance, as to what sort of foods they didn't like or couldn't eat. Clara thought it was disgusting that their friend's parents didn't do the same.

"so, we are ordering for four Kevin."

"ok. Start placing the order and I will bring the card through."

With the modern era relying on technology. The Dwyer family embraced it. They didn't do cash payments and picking up the food. It was easier for them to deliver. They weren't worried, if it cost an extra couple of pounds to have it brought directly to their front door. Clara dialled the number for the local Chinese restaurant. After all it was Williams favourite. Kevin brought the card into the kitchen and placed it on the counter in front of her and within an hour the food had arrived, and they were all eating at the table.

William picked up a spare rib and started to wave it around in front of Charlotte. He laughed "they took this rib out, while they were at it."

Kevin almost choked on his spoonful of rice. He coughed, spraying fragments across the table. This made them all burst out in fits of laughter. Clara, starting to pick up the loose grains of rice from around the table. Struggling to concentrate, she found rice everywhere. She didn't expect there to be any at the far end of the table, but it was there. It lay in between the lacework of the tablecloth. Clara decided to give up and wait until they had finished. She would then have the chance to clean it all up properly.

William continued to make them all laugh with his jokes about his procedure, until dinner was finished. With all the dishes cleared up, washed and put away. The children had returned to their rooms, leaving Kevin and Clara downstairs watching the television.

They had placed a plate of biscuits on the coffee table and either side of the plate, they had placed their mugs of coffee.

They were watching a travel show about Greece and the islands.

"not long now!"

"no. in a way I can't wait."

"what do you mean, in a way?"

"I'm just worried about William and the dreams."

"look, let's just worry about that if anything happens. We are a family and will go through this as a family."

"I know. I'm worrying too much."

Kevin kissed her on the cheek. "it will be fine." and they continued to sit and watch the show.

At ten o'clock. They were both too tired to stay up. Kevin went upstairs to check on the children, while Clara took the mugs and plate into the kitchen.

She placed the plate and mugs into the dishwasher and closed the door. She switched of the light and walked down the hallway to check the front door was locked. When she walked out of the kitchen, she hadn't noticed a tiny black face staring at her through the window, its antennae waving in the darkness.

Sleep was easy for her for the next two days. Clara had no more bad dreams, and this confused her a little. All this time. Her little visitor sat and watched. Hidden in the bushes by the kitchen window.

Chapter 10.

The morning of their holiday arrived, and the house was in total pandemonium. The four of them were running around here and there. Checking and double checking everything before the taxi arrived to pick them up for the trip to the airport.

On the dining room table, lay the passports and travel papers. Sitting in the hallway, the suitcases and carry-on bags lay in wait.

Kevin had turned off all the plugs to any electrical appliance downstairs.

"kids!"

There was a slight rumbling above Kevin's head. "yes dad" they both called back in unison.

"can you switch off all your plugs in your rooms please?"

"ok" and with another rumble, they ran back into their rooms. Kevin and Clara could hear the plugs being turned off and then being pulled out of the sockets. Moments later, they came down the stairs and into the living room. They plopped onto the sofa and sat patiently waiting.

Kevin looked at his watch. "right. the taxi will be here in five minutes. So, we need to check we have everything."

"check!" Clara called as she walked into the room.

"ok. Passports!" Clara placed her hand over them. "check!"

"booking forms!" "check!"

"money!" Clara laughed. "check. Too much!" whenever they went away, Kevin always took responsibility of the finances. He would always take plenty for the whole family, so, he could guarantee they all had a good time. From his research, there was plenty to do and more than enough restaurants to eat at.

The taxi pulled up outside and panic ensued. They were all running backwards and forwards. Stumbling in the hallway, putting shoes and coats on.

Kevin opened the front door and began taking the cases down to the car. Clara picked up all the documents off the table and placed them in her bag. The children were ready and were standing by the taxi.

"is there anything else left to come out?" Kevin called back to the house.

"we have everything, and we are good to go!" she replied.

She closed the door, placed they key into the lock and turned the key. With the house locked up, she walked down and joined the children. William opened the car door and jumped into the back seat, followed by Charlotte. They placed their belts over their shoulders and waited patiently. Their little friend watched from his new position on the garage roof.

The driver closed the boot down, walked round to his door and got in. Kevin and Clara sat down and shut the doors. Minutes later they were on their way to the airport.

They noticed that the airport was very busy. Cars, taxi's and buses were coming and going out of the terminal. People walking in and out of the main doors. Some running, some taking their time. Clara looked at their documents. They were an hour earlier than they needed to be, but that gave them plenty of time to get something to eat before they got on the plane. She wasn't keen on inflight food, so was happy being that one hour earlier. They can check in and go find a restaurant to have something decent to eat before they leave.

They said goodbye to the taxi driver and entered the terminal. William skipped through the doors first and stopped in the main hall. He looked around, amazed at the sight. He never thought one place could be so busy. "wow!" he called out. Clara placed her hand on his shoulder. "lots of people here eh!"

"is it always this busy mummy?"

"not normally sweety. But please stay close. We don't want to lose you in here!" and she gently pushed him in the direction of the check in desks. They approached the desk. Clara withdrew all the documents they needed and stood in the queue. "next please" came a voice from behind the desk. They stepped forward and Clara placed the papers onto the counter. The clerk picked them up and opened them up. checked the passports and placed them back on the counter.

"luggage please!"

Kevin placed the suitcases onto the belt. The clerk placed tags around the handle and with a whirring noise, the bags zoomed through a curtained passage and were gone.

"thank you! Next!" the clerk called out again.

'rude!' Clara thought and turned around to see an amused facial expression from Kevin.

They walked to the security desk. Once there, they amused themselves playing a game with the children. Kevin wanted to see who could be the fastest to place all their things into the trays for the x-ray machine. William laughed and won instantly. He only had his rucksack with a book and his iPad inside. Charlotte struggled to start with. She had plenty in her bag. She started to get annoyed and simply tipped the entire contents into the tray and shoved it onto the belt. Kevin and Clara were in hysterics.

Moments later, they were through the x-ray machine and picking up their belongings on the other side of the check point. Soon, they arrived at the departure lounge. A huge expanse of shops and restaurants lay before them.

Kevin started looking for a restaurant. He was getting hungry and he believed the others were too. "ok. Who wants what?"

They stood looking around.

Clara had a good idea what William and Kevin were likely to have, but she wasn't sure about Charlotte. She was getting body conscious and wondered if she would go for something light. She was surprised when Charlotte made a suggestion that shocked them all.

"as this holiday is for William. I think it should be his choice" she said.

Kevin was impressed. "burger!" William shouted, jumping on the spot.

Clara smiled. "burger it is then!" and they headed towards the burger bar at the centre of the hall.

With all the food eaten. They had made their way to a large seating area and sat facing a large screen. Flight information flashed on and off, their bright yellow lettering flickering. Kevin scrolled down to find the flight they were leaving on. A few lines down and there it was. No information was displayed, apart from the flight number and destination. "what was the flight time?" Kevin asked.

Clara opened the booking papers. "midday" she replied.

Kevin looked at his watch. "ooh! We should be boarding soon."

It had just gone eleven. He expected that they would be heading to a departure gate any moment. Clara nudged Kevin and pointed to the screen. He looked up 'gate 34' flashed next to their flight information.

"yay! Let's go!" he called, and they all rose from their seats. William began skipping again. Charlotte stayed by Clara's side until they reached their departure gate. Once there, they sat down again and waited for the call to board the plane. William stood by the window looking out onto the tarmac. He was amazed at the scene outside. Planes were everywhere he looked. People in bright orange jackets were walking around. Some loading the suitcases. Some driving small trucks around. One man was connecting the gangway to their plane. He looked up, straight at William. He gave a smile and a little wave. He waved back and turned towards Kevin. "daddy, the man down there just waved at me."

Kevin just nodded. "cool."

A member of staff came through a door and stood behind a small podium. She raised a long stick microphone.

A two-toned beeping sounded out. The next sound was the lady behind her desk calling everyone forward to board the plane. All disabled and families were to go first. Then she would call all the other passengers forward. Kevin, Clara and the children got up and walked over to the podium. They were the first in the queue. Clara passed the stewardess their paperwork and passports. They were checked and passed back to her and they were allowed to go through.

They walked along a passageway which led down to the ground floor. They walked through a set of doors to an ear-piercing sound, the engines of the aircraft. William placed his hands over his ears as they walked towards the aircraft. He hopped up onto the first step of the stairs, looking around as he did. He was fascinated be everything going on around him. At the top of the stairway a steward was standing in the doorway, welcoming them aboard.

Clara passed him the boarding cards and he signalled to another steward, who directed them to their seats.

It wasn't long before the other passengers were on board. The doors had been closed and they were all listening to the steward's safety demonstration. William was more interested in his iPad, while Charlotte had taken a book out of her bag, tucked the bag under her seat and sat reading. They had heard the safety procedures many times before and they hadn't really changed. Clara always pretended to fall asleep for the duration. Kevin always just sat there, amusing himself by looking around and spotting who wasn't paying attention.

The plane began to move. The tug, pushing it towards the taxi route.

The sound from the engines gently increased in pitch as the pilot powered them up. then it began to move forward under its own power. After a couple of minutes, the aircraft turned and then stopped.

"he we go!" Kevin whispered into Williams ear.

William gripped the arm rests. This was his least favourite part of flying. Then they were thrust into their seats, as the engines were put into full power and shot forward. Moments later, they were in the air and climbing to the cruising altitude. William now relaxed and released his grip on the arms. He picked up his iPad and began playing a game. Charlotte continued reading her book, every now and then, she looked around at her brother, Kevin and Clara. The journey to Corfu was relaxed. William had the window seat. Every now and then he would glance out of the window and scan below the plane. Looking through the gaps in the clouds.

Every now and then he would ask Kevin what it was he could see. Kevin would lean over and look. He couldn't really see much. At one point he could see the alps. The towns and villages nestled in the valleys. He sometimes wished they were lower, so he could take photos.

Sitting behind them was another family. The children were roughly the same age as William and Charlotte. The father had been cracking jokes all through the flight and as they drew closer to landing, his jokes got ever more extreme.

The captain had announced that they would be landing in around thirty minutes. This caused the father behind to crack what he thought was his best joke yet. What he didn't realise, was that his son wouldn't see it as a joke and reduced him to tears.

Kevin couldn't resist eavesdropping on what he was saying.

"here! If we overshoot the runway, your mum is going to be shopping sooner than she thought" and started to laugh. His son was confused by this comment.

"what do you mean daddy?" he replied.

"the runway is right next to the town. If we come in too fast, we will end up crashing into the town." His laughter getting louder, and his son started to cry.

Kevin started to feel a deep sense of sympathy towards the rest of this man's family. He couldn't understand why he would do something like that to deliberately scare his son. He turned his head to see if he could see the man's wife. 'why hadn't she stepped in and stopped him?' he thought. He caught a brief glimpse of her. she was asleep. Totally unaware of what he was doing.

He took the flight magazine out of the flap in the seat in front of him and began to flick through the pages. He stopped when he came across a picture of Corfu airport. The picture had been taken at a restaurant that overlooked it. The full length of the runway stretched from one side to the other, the airport terminal building sat to the right. Kevin's eyes opened wide. At the far end of the runway, he could see various buildings. Shops and apartments lay across the end of the airport. The man was right, but Kevin still couldn't understand why he would say it.

He looked at William. Worried that he may have also heard the comment.

Fortunately, he hadn't heard. He was still playing games and trying look out of the window.

Over their heads, the seatbelt sign illuminated, followed by a crescendo of seatbelts being clicked into place. People began running back to their seats. "cabin crew prepare for landing" the captain called out. The stewards walked down the aisle, making sure all the tables were back in their positions and everyone's seatbelts were on.

The plane dipped and the airbrakes activated, slowing it down. With a bump, the rear wheels contacted the runway. William watched as other passengers' heads surged forward. The force of the plane slowing down, didn't affect the forward momentum of their bodies. One at a time, he watched as people moved back into their seats.

A few people clapped and cheered. Kevin laughed. It was as if they were lucky to of landed safely. The people cheering the captain's ability not to crash into the town.

The aircraft turn and slowed further as it approached the terminal building. People began removing their seatbelts. One or two people had got out of their seats and started to remove their bags from the overhead lockers. They came to a halt, prompting everyone else to do the same.

Although they were all heading in the same direction and they would all still have to wait in the queues for passport control and the baggage hall. They still insisted on turning it into a race. Some desperate to get out and through the airport so they could have their fix of nicotine. A three-hour flight was too long for them and their lungs were screaming for salvation.

Kevin and Clara couldn't have cared less. They were in no hurry. They had no transfer waiting for them. They had prebooked a hire car. They used that method for the first time the previous year in Turkey. They got their car and arrived at the apartment complex two hours before the others from their flight arrived. They were laughing as they arrived on a coach and walking into the complex, while William and Charlotte were splashing about in the pool. The confused look on the faces of the new arrivals was a picture. They decided that this was their way in the future. When Kevin booked the flights, his next port of call was a car hire firm and have a car waiting for them.

With passport control out of the way, they made their way into the baggage hall. Their suitcases were already on the conveyor belt, going round in circles. Kevin grabbed each one and placed them down on the floor beside him. Only the children's suitcase was left. He looked at the far end of the belt, just as it came slowly round the band into view. Kevin waited for it to get to him and he gripped the handle and tugged. As he did, one side of the handle came away from the case, sending Kevin sprawling backwards. Clara grabbed what was left of the suitcase and lifted it off the belt. "looks like we will need to get another case before we go home" and started to laugh as Kevin got his composure.

With bags and cases in hand, the Dwyer family headed towards the exit, towards the car hire centre.

Kevin approached the desk and waited for someone to appear. He looked at the other desks. There were no staff on any of them. A small podgy man walked over and greeted Kevin. Moments later, with the car keys in his hand, Kevin was escorted to the parking lot where the hire cars were all lined up and ready for their clients. The man working the desk had returned inside the building.

They placed their cases in the boot and got into the car and left the parking lot and the airport. All this time they were being watched. Sitting in a bush on a waxy leaf, was Clara's little black friend. Again, his antennae waving in a semaphore fashion.

The Journey took an hour. Clara and William admired the scenery, whilst Charlotte was busy on her phone. She had turned it back on after the flight and was waiting for the services to resume. She wanted to let Sarah know they had arrived safely.

"look at that!" Kevin shouted.

They all looked straight ahead. In front of them, a small mountain range loomed in sight. Rock formations jutting out the sides, roads winding up and over the top.

As the car climbed up the roads, they drove passed a monastery, Kevin slowed down, so they could have a good look. William was looking in the other direction. As the road led higher up the mountain, the view in the opposite direction had caught Williams eye. Below them were large olive groves, towns and villages. The higher they got, the more he could see. Even Charlotte had paused her concentration on her phone, to open her camera app and take a few pictures of the scenery. The road levelled out at the top. Kevin saw a small layby and pulled in. he wanted the opportunity to admire the scenery. Once stopped he got out and stood by the side of the road. The rest of the family joined him. They hadn't noticed how hot it was when they left the airport. The cars air conditioning was already on, so it remained cool inside. Now they were out of the car, they could feel the heat. It was hot and dry.

Kevin shielded his eyes, so he could get a better look at the view.

They returned to the car and Kevin began to drive. Kevin's satellite navigation was perfect. Every turn led them in the right direction. Charlottes phone beeped to signify that it was now active once more.

She typed into the messenger and went back to taking more photos. it beeped and she went back to her messenger. Sarah had replied wishing them all a great holiday.

Soon, they found themselves entering the town of Sidari. Both sides of the road were littered with restaurants, bars and shops. The sides of the road were mostly devoid of footpaths. People walked along the road being careful of their footing, whilst others, strolled carefree and not worrying about any metal menace that could end up putting them in hospital.

"look!" Kevin pointed. Their gaze went forward.

"look at what?"

"there! The car!"

In front of them heading towards them, was a big black car with British number plates. A couple were sitting in the front. A dog's head poking out the side window. The breeze making his ears flap in the wind.

"the dog looked happy! Do you reckon they drove all the way here?" William asked.

Kevin sniggered "of course. It would have taken them a few days though."

"would you do that dad?" Charlotte asked.

"maybe when we are older, and you guys have left home" he replied.

"ooh, I think I would like that" William added.

They reached a crossroads and Kevin began to turn to the right. it was a fairly tight turn, which caused him to be cautious and he was right to be. As he cleared the turn, a black and orange beach buggy, came zooming round the corner, causing Kevin to slam on the breaks.

Had he of been seconds later, they would have been involved in a head on collision on their first day there.

"phew. That was lucky!" and he sighed. William and Charlotte were frozen solid with fear.

Kevin pulled away mumbling to himself and cursing the idiots in the buggy.

As they cleared the turn, a small bridge appeared in front of them. Beyond that, they could see a beach. It sprawled out in front of them. It seemed to be endless, as far as their eyes could see. Kevin checked his mirrors and slowed down so they could all enjoy the sight.

Peddle boats lined the shore. Some had slides on the top. Kevin pointed to them. "we could hire one of those. Fancy that kids?"

William got excited "yeah, yeah, yeah!" he screamed.

Clara turned "ok William. Calm down. we have plenty of time to hire one!"

"sorry mummy" and he clapped his hands. He wanted to do so much while they were there.

As they went further along the road, they came to a walled off area. The walls were at least ten feet tall. Clara could see a stone cross poking over. Clara looked slightly confused. As she followed the wall, she noticed that it was built right to the edge of the shoreline.

"why would they build a cemetery right up to the shore? Surely in bad weather that would all collapse into the sea" she asked.

Kevin agreed. To him, it seemed a little silly. He wondered the same thing. as they passed William noticed the gates to the cemetery were open. Inside, he could see the graves. Their marker stones rising above the ground. Some towering over others.

One grave had a cherub overlooking the grave, as if it were guarding it. Its hand cupped together. In its hands, William could see a dark shape.

It was the cricket that had taken up residence outside their kitchen and watched them leave. The same cricket that sat in the bush outside the airport and watched as they got in their hire car and drove away. Now it was there in the cemetery, watching them again. Neither William nor the others had seen it. William didn't think anything of it and turned his gaze to the beach.

As they travelled a little further up the road, a signpost came into view. A brown sign with a palm tree on it read. 'MEGALI LUXURIES'

"that's where we are heading."

Clara suddenly froze as Kevin slowed down at a junction.

She recognised the surroundings. The tavernas, restaurants and even that section of the beach were all too familiar. These were all in her dreams. The section of beach clearly the same. It was where William and herself had to stand and wait until the crickets had left.

The only difference in what she was currently seeing and what she had seen in the dreams, were the amount of people. There were people everywhere. The tavernas and restaurants were bursting at the seams. The beach was full of people. Some sunbathing, others splashing about and swimming in the blue waters. Kevin turned the car to the right and advanced down a small road. Clara's gaze fixed ahead. This was the road that her and William had walked down after they left the tunnel. The road that the army of crickets had followed them down. The crickets would be the last thought before Kevin broke her out of her chain of thought.

"babes. We are here!"

"uh! What! Ah right" she replied blinking and shaking her head to try and remove the thoughts.

He turned into the driveway and into another world. The drive was brick paved, the parking bays all clearly marked. Down either side, were shrubs of varying colours. Clara pushed all the thoughts out. She was determined that this was not going to affect their holiday.

Kevin pulled into one of the bays. Next to a red pick-up truck. The words fire department were written down the side. Kevin exited the car and stood by the side of it with his hands on his hips.

"Kali Mera!" came a voice from by the pool. A smallish man came walking out from behind a pile of sunbeds and headed towards Kevin.

He stopped and held out his hand. Kevin shook it. They stood talking for a while. The man walked to the pick-up and retrieved a key from the front seat and handed it to Kevin. He then started walking to a set of stairs on the side of one of the buildings.

Kevin came back to the car. "ok guys. This is it. Leave the bags here. The owner is going to show us around and then we can worry about the bags."

William was the first to jump out. his excitement showing as he skipped and jumped towards Kevin.

Clara decided to be cautious. Most of what she could see was identical to her dreams. The pool, the edges or the wall surrounding the apartments. The flowers and shrubs. Everything was the same. This alarmed her. but she had now learned to deal with it. she caught up with Kevin and William, just as they reached the stairs.

Fanis, the owner, was standing in the doorway at the top waiting for them. As they got closer, he opened the door.

"welcome to Megali Luxuries!" he said politely, and they entered the property.

The tour of the apartment took a mere five minutes. He explained how everything worked. What days the rubbish would be collected and gave Clara his contact number in case they needed anything else.

With that, he wished them a lovely holiday and left the apartment.

Clara opened her bag and took out some various sachets. She opened one of the cupboards, found two mugs and placed them on the counter. She opened the fridge and peered inside.

The owner had left them a large bottle of water, which she used to fill up the kettle. Emptied a couple of the sachets into the mugs and stood waiting for the kettle to boil.

Kevin went back out to the car to fetch the bags and suitcases. He struggled with His and Clara's suitcase, but the children's cases were easier and got them up the stairs with ease. William had sat himself on the balcony looking out towards the pool. He wanted to jump in right away, but the family had a protocol. They didn't do anything until all bags were unpacked and Kevin and Clara had had a cup of tea or coffee.

The double doors further down the balcony opened and Charlotte walked out. she saw William sitting at the table and walked over.

"looks good doesn't it?"

"yeah! Can't wait to jump into the pool" he replied.

"if you put your stuff away, mum and dad may let us go in for a while."

William pushed his chair back and walked into the room, to start unpacking. Charlotte sat down and looked at her phone. The picture Sarah had sent her, was taken in the exact spot that she was sitting in at that very moment.

she looked towards the kitchen where Clara was making the drinks. "hey mum. This is the same apartment that Sarah and her folks stayed in when they were here!"

"really?"

"yeah. I'm sitting in the same place Sarah took her photo from."

Clara came out onto the balcony and picked up Charlottes phone.

"oh yeah! have you told Sarah?"

"yes. I sent her a message, but she hasn't seen it yet." Clara placed the phone back down in front of her and walked back into the apartment to sort her clothes out. she hadn't seen the plot of land next door and would worry her if she had.

Chapter 11.

With all the unpacking complete, Kevin and Clara were discussing what they were going to do for dinner. William and Charlotte were sitting at the table on the balcony. William was playing on his iPad and Charlotte had immersed herself back into her book again.

"shall I go and ask dad if we can go to the pool? They can watch out over us from up here" William asked.

"ok" Charlotte replied. With that William got up and walked in to ask.

Moments later Kevin came out and looked towards the pool. He stood and thought for a minute. Charlotte was responsible and often looked after her brother. Now was slightly different. William wasn't allowed to get his head wet for another three days.

"ok. But please make sure your brother doesn't get his head wet please."

"of course, dad" She replied, and she ran into the bedroom to get changed. William didn't need to get changed. He had conveniently put his swimming shorts on. All he had to do was take his shirt off and jump in.

Charlotte returned wearing her swimming costume and wrapped in a towel. "come on then dude. Let's go!"

Clara watched them leave as she sat at the table indoors, sorting out her make-up. Kevin was sitting on the balcony watching them walk over to the pool. Charlotte ran over to the far end of the pool and dived in headfirst. Seconds passed and her head bobbed up through the water and she swam over to the shallow end where William had jumped in and was wading around.

With everything of hers unpacked and away in drawers. Clara picked up her drink and walked out to join Kevin.

She placed her mug down on the table and sat down with her back facing the pool. She knew Kevin was watching the children.

"what would you like to do for dinner?" she asked.

"ooh. I think we should find a lovely traditional Greek place. Somewhere where they do the dancing and that!" he replied.

"sounds perfect."

"we'll give the children an hour, and then we will get ready to go!"

Clara laid back in the chair and closed her eyes. "ok." She felt comfortable with the suns heat beaming onto the balcony. She felt strange. Part of her expected to close her eyes and get another vision, but not this time. She could still make out the light through her eyelids. No sounds or strange sights and certainly no crickets.

She smiled. With the comfort, she felt that she could enjoy the holiday now. Most of her fears had gone. There was still a slight issue that kept mulling over in her mind. Why did she dream this location?

With the sun starting to set, the children returned to the apartment and each in turn, had a shower and got dressed for their evening out.

Kevin and Clara had taken it in turns to get changed, while the other watched the children in the pool, so they were ready.

Twenty minutes passed and they were ready.

The plan would be to walk into the town and have a look around first, before choosing a restaurant. Kevin wanted to find the church and see why Sidari was so highly recommended. They left the complex and started walking down the road towards the beach. In front of them, on the horizon. The sun had created a beautiful scene of colour. The mountains of Albania silhouetted against the changing colours of the sky. They arrived at the crossroads and stood on the seawall, staring out to sea. In the distance they could see a ferry, slowly moving, heading south. The lights bright and shimmering in the enveloping darkness.

The lights on the mainland also shimmered. The air so clear enabled them to see with clarity. They turned and walked down the road. William tugged on Kevin's arm. "can I walk along the beach daddy?"

Kevin looked down. "sorry son. Not in those shoes."

Moments later, they had reached the town. The main street full of people. Cars driving through were taking care as they passed by. Every building was covered in various lights. Staff were standing outside almost every bar and restaurant, trying to entice passers-by inside.

"can we go in here please dad?" and Charlotte pointed to a bar.

Kevin looked. The bar Charlotte wanted them to go into had a lady Gaga tribute act in that evening.

"honey, we are looking for somewhere to have dinner. We are here for two weeks. We have plenty of time for those things."

Charlotte was disappointed but accepted what she was told.

The smells coming from the restaurants were making Kevin's mouth water. The different foods, creating different smells, merging together and wafting down the main road. Finally, they reached the heart of the town. The centre being the church. They all stopped and looked into the grounds. The church had been decorated by different coloured lights. Casting beams in all directions. Kevin could see the church priest walking around and chatting with people. They could hear children running around in the play area towards the rear of the gardens.

Kevin admired the spirit of the community. They all stood or sat chatting with each other. Something he rarely saw at home.

They carried on walking. They passed the church and round to more businesses. They saw Fanis the owner of the complex chatting to customers in a shop.

"blimey, he gets around a bit, doesn't he? Fire chief, landlord and shop owner. Wow!" Kevin quipped.

"what about here Kevin?" Clara called.

To his right. set back from the main path was a walkway through to a beautifully decorated restaurant. It advertised Greek traditional food with Greek traditional entertainment. In the entrance lay an a-board displaying the menu. It was full of different dishes. And nestled at the bottom, a section of English dishes. Kevin turned his nose up to those. He wanted Proper Greek food.

"ok. Here will do" and they walked in.

A young waiter raced down to greet them. He wished them a good evening and asked how many people there were dining. He then escorted them to a table, where he seated Clara and Charlotte. He then appeared with a handful of menus. Distributed them around the table and walked away. Moments later he returned with a basket of fresh bread and a humus dip.

"now this is what I call traditional" and Kevin took the first piece of bread. This signalled the children to do the same and they each took some.

The waiter returned to take their order. They were struggling to decide on what to have. But after a while. They had cracked it. they were all going to try something different and try each other's food.

An hour passed. The food had arrived quickly, and they tucked in. as they sat having coffee, Charlotte noted that the sun had gone down completely and apart from the lights in the distance. It was almost pitch-black outside.

They paid the bill and walked out of the rear of the restaurant. They walked down a lightly decked walkway and onto the beach.

"you can take your shoes off here William!"

They all took their shoes off and made their way to the shoreline. They could hear the waves lapping up onto the sand. As their feet contacted the water, they could feel the sand seeping between their toes. William thought it tickled and it made him giggle. After a long day traveling and a hearty meal, Kevin and Clara were ready for an early night.

Finally, they were back at the complex. It was lit up like the church. All around the edges of the grass, lay small lights casting colours in every direction. The swimming pool lights were also on, illuminating the water with a blue glow. They climbed up the steps to the apartment and within minutes of opening the door, they were all inside and ready for bed.

With the children in bed, Kevin and Clara made a cup of coffee and sat out on the balcony.

"what do you reckon on a day at the beach tomorrow?" Clara finally asked.

"sounds like a plan."

"I will need to go to the shop round the corner for some groceries first. Then we can head out then."

Kevin was happy with the plan. The got a few things from the shop on the way back that evening. But it wouldn't have been enough for lunches and snacks during the day.

They finished their drinks and went to bed. Minutes after Kevin's head rested on the pillow, he as fast asleep. Clara laid there staring at the ceiling. The day had been long for all of them. She should have been tired, but she just couldn't sleep. In the distance, very faintly, she could hear a cricket chirping. This stopped her getting any sleep for a few hours. The sound remained distant. It never got louder, which to her meant it wasn't getting closer. She finally drifted to sleep.

The following day started abruptly. Clara was woken by the children.

"mummy! Mummy! Come outside. Look at this!" Clara opened her eyes, but it was her ears that alarmed her first. the noise was deafening. Kevin stirred then sat up in the bed rubbing his eyes. "what the hell is that noise?" he shouted. "I can hardly hear myself think."

"outside. Come look." Charlotte shouted and she opened the balcony doors. The sunlight came in, lighting the room.

Clara got out of bed, headed over to the dressing table. She put on her dressing gown and her slippers and walked out to where Charlotte and William were standing.

"look mum" Charlotte said and pointed to the plot of land next door.

Clara froze. The sight confirmed what she could hear. In the middle of the plot, was what she could only describe as a pile of rocks, similar to the one in her dream. This one was different. She took a step forward. When she focused again, it was the same pile, only it was covered in a thick black blanket of crickets. they were writhing and crawling all over. She couldn't see where they were coming from.

She ran back into the room, where Kevin was just getting dressed. She startled him, as he was putting his feet through the legs of his shorts. He stumbled back and landed on the bed.

"they are here Kevin!" she shouted. "they are outside."

Kevin got up and rushed to the balcony. "oh my god! They are real!"

"What the hell do we do?"

"I don't think there is much we can do, apart from getting the hell out of here" Clara replied.

Kevin was a little confused. "cannot we try to understand what is happening? I mean. This is linked to you and William."

"I'm scared of what may happen Kevin."

He took hold of Clara's hands. "apart from the fact they looked scary. Did they make you feel in danger? After all, you said they only followed you."

"not just that! the first time I saw William in the dreams, they were crawling into his mouth."

"but that could mean something else. Not necessarily that they mean harm to us."

Clara was more confused now than she was before.

They walked out onto the balcony, where William and Charlotte still stood watching the crickets. A few had dispersed, leaving gaps between them, exposing the rocks beneath. The sound had also dimmed. Clara hadn't noticed her little friend, sitting at the far end. Instead of watching them, it was facing the rocks.

William spotted it and slowly walked over with the intention of catching him.

Clara went back inside, making her miss what was about to happen.

As William approached the cricket turned and looked directly at him. "hello buddy!" William softly spoke. "why are you not down there with the others?" and he held out his hand. He wasn't scared at all. he smiled as the cricket slowly stepped onto his hand and rested on his palm. Charlotte saw William with the cricket and walked over.

The cricket just sat there looking at William. When Charlotte approached, its gaze changed from him and was directed at her.

"he looks cute!" she remarked.

As she spoke, the crickets head tilted sideways as if it understood what she had said. It raised its hind legs and gently rubbed them together and it made the chirping sound.

"you better put him down. if mum hears that and comes out, she will go nuts!"

William agreed and put him back down on the brickwork. His new friend tilted his head sideways. He didn't want to leave him. "it's ok little buddy. I will see you later." And the cricket chirped back and hopped off the balcony.

"that's weird William. But cool at the same time."

Kevin had been watching but didn't get involved. He could see William wasn't in any danger. One cricket wouldn't be able to take out a little boy and his sister. He was amazed at the communication between them.

It was almost as if the cricket was a pet to William.

Clara returned after getting dressed. She walked onto the balcony and looked out across to the rocks. "where did they go?" she asked. Kevin lifted his gaze towards the land next door. They had all gone. There was just grass and the pile of rocks in the centre. There wasn't one cricket anywhere. They couldn't even hear the chirping.

"I don't know. I was watching William and Charlotte at the other end there" and he pointed to the far end of the balcony.

Charlotte grabbed her bag. "I'm heading to the shop. Does anyone want to come with me?" she asked.

Both the children remained tight lipped. They wanted to go into the pool again. "ok. I will go on my own. Bye "and she headed towards the door.

"bye mum" William called out. they watched her appear at the bottom of the steps and walk down the path past the pool. "bye mum!" Charlotte shouted across the complex. Clara turned and waved as she walked out and down the road.

"can we go down to the pool dad?" William asked. he expected the answer to be no. but he thought there wouldn't be any harm in asking.

"of course, you can" Kevin replied, "just make sure that as soon as your mother gets back, you come out."

"ok" and they shot into the apartment, grabbed a towel each and raced out the door. Kevin watched as the ran across the grass to the pool. He walked into the kitchen and poured himself a glass of fruit juice and returned to the balcony and put his feet up. Sipping his juice, he watched the world go by. Every now and then, he would check to make sure the children were ok. A fruit merchant pulled into the driveway. His voice calling out through a speaker describing the different fruit he had for sale. He noticed Charlotte looking up at him. He waved and shook his head "no we don't want anything!" he called back. It was almost as if the merchant heard and understood. The vans reverse light went out and it stopped moving.

He sat there for a few minutes, then pulled forward and out of the complex. His speaker being heard as he drove off into the distance.

Kevin noticed William at the side of the pool. He was looking at one of the sunbeds. His cricket friend had returned. Charlotte was swimming around in circles at the far end of the pool.

William was talking to the cricket. from where Kevin was on the balcony, he could just make out the cricket's head tilting from one side to the other. he got up out of the chair and walked into the apartment. He grabbed the key and went down to the poolside. As he walked over to the pool. The cricket hopped round to face him. William muttered something and the cricket hopped back.

Kevin sat by the side of the pool and dangled his feet into the water.

"you found a friend son!"

"yeah dad. He's cool, Can I take him home?"

Kevin thought this was hysterical "sorry buddy. I don't think he would survive the journey."

This upset William a little. "sorry, you can't home with us!"

Kevin was a little freaked out by this. His son was talking to an insect and the insect understood what he was saying. There was now a conflict in his head. Should he tell Clara about this or just leave it. after a few moments he decided that it would be best to tell her. but he would have to wait until the children are doing something away from them, so he couldn't be disturbed.

He knew Clara would want answers, he wanted answers. For a moment he thought about what he wanted William to ask. He didn't want things to be too complicated. So, he thought of questions that would be simple.

"William! Can you ask it a couple of questions for me?"

"yes dad. Ok!"

"can you ask him, if he and his friends mean to hurt you?"

"ok!" and he repeated the question to the cricket.

The crickets head tilted, and it raised it legs again. It chirped a few times, then lowered its legs down.

"he says no. they don't mean me or us any harm. They won't hurt us dad!"

Kevin's mind went blank as Clara walked into the complex with shopping bags in her hands. He got up from the poolside and started to walk towards her. he briefly looked at William. "don't say anything to your mother!" then he looked at Charlotte. "that goes for you too. Your mum won't understand at the moment."

Charlotte nodded "ok dad. No worries!"

He walked over to Clara, reaching out to take one of the bags. It was fairly heavy, and he was surprised, that she brought that much. The opportunity to talk to Clara would be now. But he wanted to think about how he was going to tell her first. so, they just talked about her shopping trip.

Clara only wanted specific items, but found herself putting one thing in the basket, then another. Before she knew it, she had gone back to the front of the store and exchanged her basket for a trolley. She then started putting more items into that. she found crisps, breakfast cereal. She felt like she was on her normal shopping routine at home and she found it hard to stop. Finally, she arrived at the till and the shop assistant started ringing the products in.

A few minutes passed and all her goods were in bags. Clara paid, picked up two bags in each hand and left the shop. She wasn't too bothered about the weight of them as she only had to walk up the road a little and she would be back. A minute or two, she regretted ever going to the shop. Her arms ached. And when Kevin went over to her and took one of the bags. She was relieved.

"ok kids?" she asked as they walked past the pool.

"yes mum!" Charlotte replied. "yup" William called back.

The afternoon was spent down at the beach. Kevin toiled and troubled about how and when he would talk to Clara about what had happened with William earlier.

At that moment, they were all happy. Clara was happy. She sat on the beach towel watching the children splashing about in the sea.

"do you fancy walking into town again tonight and maybe try that restaurant next to the church? San what's it's face!" he couldn't remember the name fully. But it looked modern and trendy. When they walked past the night before, he noticed it was very popular.

"you mean San Remo's!" and she laughed.

"then after we could pop into one of the bars and have a drink or two before we go back to the apartment!"

Clara loved the idea. But she wanted to make sure it wasn't a rowdy bar full of drunks.

"ok. We will do that! but it has to be a decent bar!"

"of course!"

William came running up the beach. "daddy. We just had fish swimming around our feet!"

Kevin got up and walked down to the water. Charlotte was staring down at her feet and laughing. Kevin walked in next to her and peered down through the water to his feet. Tiny fish swam up to him and darted between them. Some stopped and nibbled at his toes. William joined in the fun and jumped in. after the sand had cleared, they stood and watched the fish.

Clara saw them having fun together and didn't want to be the odd one out. she got up and walked down to join them. She took a few steps, stubbed her toe on a pebble and lurched forward. Kevin held out his arms stopping her from diving headfirst into the water.

She gained her composure and stood straight. The all looked at each other and they all burst out laughing.

They all stayed at the beach for a couple of hours. William was starting to get a little bored. He had built himself a sandcastle and decorated it with stones and pebbles. Charlotte had retreated to her beach towel and was trying to catch a tan. Clara had pulled a book out of her bag and was attempting to read it, but Kevin would distract her every now and then, by getting up and trying to tempt her into the water for a swim.

He walked out of the sea and sat down." the water is starting to get cold. I think we should head back soon and get ready for dinner."

Clara looked at her watch and agreed. "yes. Its four o'clock already!" she tapped Charlotte on the shoulder "c'mon you. We are going to head back now!"

Charlotte lifted herself up and started to put her belongings back in her bag.

"William buddy. Come up now. We are heading back!" Kevin called down the beach. "ok dad. Coming!" he got up off the sand and jumped into his masterpiece, destroying all his hard work and ran up towards them.

That evening, they walked round the other side of the town. It was all the same. Bars holding tribute acts and restaurants boasting traditional entertainment along with traditional foods. They walked back towards the church. Outside the gates, street vendors sat, selling their wares. An artist creating caricatures of passers-by, who laughed as he exposed his craft to his wanting clients. By the entrance to the church sat a lady creating colourful hair braids. Parents standing close by admiring the skill and craftmanship.

The lights of Kevin's chosen restaurant stood out from all the others. Bright red and blue neon bulbs illuminated the street.

As they got closer, Clara spotted the perfect place to go after they had finished their food. Opposite the church, sat a small bar. Tv screens were showing sports and music was being played at a low level. Clara nodded to herself. 'this is the place we need to come to!' she thought.

Inside, were plenty of customers. Mostly families and older couples. The atmosphere was relaxed and calm.

They stepped into the restaurant and instantly a server came out of nowhere making Clara jump.

"hello people. Just the four of you?" he asked with a smile.

"yes" Kevin replied, and the server strolled away with the Dwyer family in tow. He stopped at a large table and signalled for them to sit. As they sat, menus flew in front of them. Kevin was surprised and laughed. "that's quick!" he whispered to Clara. For the next five minutes, they sat scanning the menu. The server returned and took their order.

Clara got a clear view along the street. As time went by, more and more people appeared. The popularity of the town was immense.

"after dinner, we can pop into that bar over there!" and she pointed across the street. Kevin looked behind him and laughed. "which one? There's plenty!" and they both laughed. Clara bobbed her head a little, so she could see the name of the bar. "the Seriani bar" she replied.

"that looks cosy! Ok. We will go in there after!"

The food arrived and was placed on the table. Neatly placed and arranged on the plates were gyros. Wraps filled with a variety of meat and salads. Kevin picked one and took a huge bite. His eyes rolled as the flavours rolled over his tongue. "oh my god! This is amazing!"

Hands plunged towards the plate and the food was gone.

For half an hour nothing was said as they enjoyed their food. Nothing remained after. Kevin was mopping up droplets of Tzatziki off the plate with what remained of the bread. "wow! We are definitely having those again" he said looking around at the agreeing faces.

They got up from the table. Kevin walked over to the counter and paid the bill, while Clara and the children stood outside on the side of the street.

Kevin re-joined them and they walked over the road into the bar. Kevin scanned the bar for a place for them to sit. As they approached, a family got up from a set of comfy bamboo chairs, waved to the barman and walked off down the street.

"Great timing!" and Clara and the children slipped into the chairs. Kevin walked up to the bar. There were a number of people standing along the bar. He didn't have to wait long before the barman skipped along to him.

"can I help?" he asked.

Kevin ordered four drinks and returned to their seats overlooking the street. The barman appeared with a tray. The children's fruit cocktail was placed in front of them, with umbrella's opened and poking out of the top of a slice of orange and a sparkler, crackling violently. Kevin wasn't a big drinker, so he only ordered half a pint of Mythos. Clara simply had a cup of coffee.

She took a sip and leaned back into the chair. "oh my god. This is better than those big coffee bars" this made the children laugh. As Clara withdrew her cup, a large frothy moustache hung off her top lip.

Charlotte pointed "you might want to use your napkin!"

"oh god!" and she picked it up off the tray and wiped it off as quickly as she could. Saving her too much embarrassment. As time moved on, so did the people and the street didn't seem so busy. William sat yawning.

"I think its best we just have the one drink and then head back!"

Clara agreed. With the drinks finished, they made a slow walk back. As with the night before, William and Charlotte, had gone straight to bed. Kevin and Clara were also tired. For the next thirty minutes, they just lay in bed chatting about the day. Kevin's eyes got heavy and he fell asleep. Clara wasn't far behind. She would have her second full night's sleep. Minutes passed and she gave in and fell asleep herself.

Chapter 12.

It was a late start. Kevin and the children were already up. William and Charlotte had eaten breakfast and getting ready to go down to the pool. Kevin sat on the balcony eating some toast and checking his emails. The heat of the day was building. He would let Clara sleep in. once they were ready, he would take the children down to the pool and wait for Clara to join them.

He could hear a cricket, but wherever he looked, he couldn't find it.

He knocked on the children's bedroom door. "you guys ready?"

"yeah" came the reply and the door opened. Charlotte and William were sitting on the bed. On the pillow was the creator of the chirping. It was William's small friend. The cricket was perched on William's pillow. He sat there chirping frantically. The children found it amusing. "he wants to know if we are going to the pool today!" William finally spoke.

Kevin was still confused. He wanted to know how his son was able to understand and talk to a bug.

"yes. We are going in a minute" he replied.

"get your things together and we will go" and he turned, shaking his head as he walked out of the room. He could hear the children laughing as he picked up the towels and took a bottle of water out of the fridge. Moments later, the children came out of the room, smiles still present on their faces.

Kevin picked up the bag of towels and opened the door. "let's go!" he whispered and closed the door as the children walked down the steps.

There weren't any others at the pool. They knew there were others staying at the complex. 'they must have gone to the beach or elsewhere' Kevin thought to himself.

He laid the towels onto the sunbeds. Leaving a place open for Clara, for when she came down. Charlotte had already jumped into the pool. Kevin called William over. He wanted to check his head. Today was the day that William would be able to finally be able to swim. William sat down on the end of the sunbed and Kevin lifted off the dressing. The area that the doctor had done the biopsy on, had healed well. Only small patches of dry blood lay matted into his hair were still present.

He lifted a tuft of hair, coated in congealed blood, exposing the area of the drill hole. It had healed quickly. He was happy to allow him into the pool.

"ok buddy, you can go swimming now. Just don't scratch that area ok?"

"yes daddy" and he ran off to the far end of the pool, where Charlotte was practicing her underwater handstands. "Jeronimo!" he shouted and leaped into the pool. Water cascaded in all directions. Charlotte resurfaced, coughing and spluttering. William had jumped in a little too close to her, surprising her in the process.

They both swam around giggling. William had found a new energy. The restrictions placed on him were gone.

Kevin was overjoyed. Seeing both children happy, relieved a lot of his worry.

Williams new friend also seemed happy. It sat on the wall, that joined with the land next door. Chirping happily.

Kevin opened the bag and reached in. he grabbed some sun cream. He wasn't keen on sun burn. He slapped it on and rubbed it in. he lifted up the back of the sunbed and laid himself back. The sun shone brightly through his eyelids. He found it unbearable, he kept having to shield his eyes. He eventually reached down for his glasses and placed them on his face.

With the children playing and having fun, Kevin relaxed. He was unaware that the cricket was beckoning the children to him. All Kevin could hear was the children's laughter and splashing of water.

"WILLIAM!" a voice screamed.

Kevin jumped up to see Clara standing on the balcony. Her eyes wide, her mouth open, screaming her sons name over and over. She was pointing to something past him.

He turned, in his mind, he could still hear the children playing in the pool. But when he faced the pool. It was still. The children were no longer there. Looking around, Kevin started to panic. His heart beating tenfold. Charlotte was on the sunbed by his side. She was asleep.

He jumped up, rubbing his eyes. He looked back to the balcony where Clara had been standing. She had gone. Seconds later she came running across the grass towards him.

"HE'S NEXT DOOR ON THE ROCKS!" she shouted.

Kevin broke out running, pushing the branches of the shrubs out of the way to get to the wall.

He put his hands on the top and shimmied himself up. then fell backwards at the sight that greeted him.

Clara ran over to him and helped to pick him up.

"THEY'VE GOT OUR BOY! GET UP!"

She pulled him off the floor and he tried again.

"NO!" he shouted, and he turned, grabbed Clara's hands and pulled her up. They sat on top of the wall and stared. Clara couldn't believe that her dreams were real. She jumped down the other side of the wall.

"WILLIAM! WILLIAM!" and she began running towards him.

A figure was standing on top of the rocks. It was William.

Amassing over his body was an army of black crickets. Clara found it hard to see any part of her son underneath this black shroud. As she reached the base, something stopped her. she was frozen on the spot. She raised her hands to push forward. Trying to break an invisible barrier that was stopping her getting to her son.

Her energy waned and her arms dropped to her side. She was powerless to stop them. She lifted her head towards William and noticed that the crickets on the back of his head were crawling round in circles. At the centre of this was a single cricket. his antennae waving in all directions.

It was sitting on top of the scab created by the biopsy.

She tried a sidestep and to her surprise, she moved. She took a few steps to her left and tried pushing forward again. It didn't work. She took a few more until the front of William came into view. She remembered in her dreams that they were swarming around his mouth and entering his body. As she came face to face with William, she could see his eyes. Nothing was going into his mouth. They just walked over his face as part of the circular movement they were all doing.

She was partly relieved, but the panic and fear were still present.

"GRAB HIM!" Kevin shouted from the wall. He had climbed down onto the grass and was making his way to her.

"I CAN'T!" she called back. "SOMETHING IS STOPPING ME!"

The more she tried to get to William, the more tired she became. By now Charlotte had woken and left the sunbed and was propping herself up between the wall and a young tree growing by the side of it.

"Mum, Dad. Its ok. They don't mean any harm!" she called.

But neither Kevin nor Clara could hear her. they were too busy calling to each other. Charlotte pushed herself over the wall and began running as fast as she could towards her mother.

Kevin reached Clara first and began trying to push forward. As with Clara, the more he pushed, the less energy he had. Frustrated and drained, he too dropped his arms to his side and watched.

Charlotte arrived at their side. "it's ok mum. They don't want to hurt him!"

Clara couldn't believe what she was hearing. Charlottes words echoing through her mind.

Kevin looked down at Charlotte. "what do you mean?" he said with an angry tone.

"I told William; I wouldn't say anything" she replied.

"you knew this was going to happen?" Clara finally spoke.

"William was talking to one of them this morning, before we came down to the pool. It said they didn't want to hurt any of us. they want to help!"

Clara started to display her anger towards Charlotte and the situation. "HELP! THIS IS HELP?" she shouted.

Kevin put his arm around her, and she buried her head into his shoulder and began to sob.

"I want my son back!" she cried.

It was as if the crickets had heard her plea. A loud chirping noise rang out. They looked up to see the circling had stopped. Slowly, they began to crawl off Williams body. They walked down to the rocks and disappeared. After minutes, there was only a lone cricket sitting on Williams shoulder. Its antennae were still.

Clara let go of Kevin and pushed her hands forward. The barrier that stopped her before, was gone. Her arms stretched out in front of her. she stepped forward and found herself able to put her leg up onto the rocks. Her energy returned and she climbed up and embraced William in her arms. The cricket had jumped off and was sitting beside them.

At first William didn't move. Clara suddenly felt something on her hips. It was Williams hands. They were moving up. she looked down and saw Williams beaming smile looking back at her.

"hi mummy!" he whispered.

A wave of emotions swept through Clara's body and she tightened her grasp.

"they helped me mummy" William said, and he looked at his friend.

Clara also looked down. the cricket sat there looking up at them.

She wasn't sure as to what they had done. But William seemed to be fine.

"he's my friend mummy. It's ok!"

She smiled at the cricket. it chirped back and jumped. As it leapt into the air, it began to break up. small fragments of its body broke away and turned to dust. Then the rest also broke up and vanished the same way. Seconds later the cricket had gone, leaving Clara and William standing on top of the pile of rocks with Kevin and Charlotte standing at the base transfixed on what they had witnessed.

Clara looked down at Kevin and smiled. He held his arms up. William jumped down into his arms and hugged him. Clara made her way down and joined them.

"are you ok?" Kevin asked. William looked at him "I'm fine."

He raised his hand to Clara "and you babes?"

She gave a confused look and a half smile "yes."

Charlotte had been looking around for a way out of the property, without having to climb back over the wall. She walked over to a small entrance. "over here!" she called out.

"thank god, I don't think I can ever go back over that wall" and he laughed.

They walked out and back into the complex. Clara and the children walked back up to the apartment, while Kevin walked over to the sunbeds and gathered up their belongings.

He joined them moments later and they sat down in the living room. William and Charlotte sat playing on William's iPad. Kevin and Clara sat side by side, watching them.

"what do we do now?" Clara asked.

"carry on with the holiday, I guess" came the reply.

That afternoon they all went out for a walk into the town.

Clara had proposed that they went to the church and had a look inside. She had a reason. She was hoping that if, what happened to William was anything nasty, then maybe the church would be able to cleanse them.

Kevin was happy with the idea. With them all calm and relaxed once more. They put on their shoes and left the apartment.

Clara felt an enormous sense of well-being as they walked down the road towards the sea. All her fears had almost gone. The only thing that was still eating at the back of her mind, was the issue of Williams test results.

The idea of the holiday was to forget momentarily of what was to possibly come. As much as she tried, it would still play on her mind every now and then.

They walked along the beach towards the town.

It seemed the town was as busy during the day, as it was at night. People and cars were moving in all directions. Delivery trucks were parked on the main road, dropping off supplies.

Clara and Charlotte decided to look in every shop they came across.

Kevin had no choice, but to follow them inside. He was the one with the money. Clara had purposely left her bag in the apartment. He didn't mind, it was their money anyway.

Eventually they arrived at the church yard. The owner of the bar opposite was sitting on the church wall with his family. They were chatting and smiling at people as they walked past. Their two boys laughing at each other's jokes, smiled at William and Charlotte as they approached. William smiled back.

They entered the grounds and made their way to the church door.

They were amazed when they walked in. the church was covered in beautiful paintings and carvings. Some made of gold.

They only spent a short time in there. Clara was now convinced, that the crickets were not nasty, evil things and that they didn't mean William any harm.

Moments later, they were sitting by the side of the bandstand looking around the garden. Clara was huddled in Kevin's arms, whilst the children played in the play area.

"do you think that's it? they won't be back?" she asked.

"I don't think so. Let's just enjoy what we have left of the holiday" he replied and that was exactly what they did.

For the remainder of their trip. They spent days touring around the island. They visited monasteries in the mountains. Took a trip down to Corfu town and spent all day walking around the shops looking for gifts for family and friends. William wanted to drag them into a mc Donald's for lunch. Kevin denied him that privilege. Instead, he found a small restaurant and they sat eating club sandwiches.

After, they spent the rest of that day walking around Corfu towns old and new forts. William and Kevin absorbed the history of them. While Clara and Charlotte wished, they were back in the shops. Clara had heard that there was a Marks and Spencer's there. They hadn't found it yet and were determined to do so.

With only a few days left, they decided they would spend the rest of the stay relaxing by the pool or on the beach. In the evenings they returned to the town for dinner. They had a favourite place to eat. A small Greek diner next to the Seriani Bar. They would eat and then go into the bar and spend the rest of the evening there.

They even made friends with the bar owners and their children. William and Charlotte had been playing pool when they came through the kitchen and into the bar area. Their youngest son, watching them eagerly. Their mum walked through with her eldest and crossed over to the church wall while her husband stood in the bar changing the channels on the tv's.

William came running over. "mummy, daddy. I've made another friend. His name is Dino!" Clara looked over to where Dino was standing and gave him a little wave.

"That's lovely sweety. Don't forget to play fair" and William walked back over and continued playing.

The owner of the complex walked into the bar and began talking with the owner. They caught his eye and walked over to them.

"have you enjoyed you're stay here?" he asked.

"loved every minute of it" Kevin replied shaking his hand.

"we will definitely be coming back" Clara added.

"that is good!" and he walked back over to the bar.

A golden retriever walked through the bar followed by the couple Kevin had seen earlier in the holiday, driving past them. They walked through to the kitchen and out the back door. Moments later, they returned and sat down at the table next to them.

They sat and chatted all evening. Kevin and Clara had made friends with a large chain of people without realising. The couple sitting with them, were the mother and father of one of the owners. The owner of the complex happened to be the godfather of one of their grandchildren. Everything was linked.

Clara felt sad, that on their last night there, they had made good friends with people. They knew they would be returning to the island and hoped they would meet them again.

The other grandson had joined William and Charlotte at the pool table and was briefly introduced as Dimitris. He quickly said "hi" and he returned to the game.

With the evening at an end, they bid farewell to their newfound friends and left the bar. They walked back along the beach. They stopped occasionally to take pictures of each other as they walked.

The following morning, it was back to a state of pandemonium. Suitcases packed in a rush and everything tidied and cleaned up.

Kevin and Clara were checking, then double checking that everything was packed and in the right place.

Kevin grabbed the cases and took them down to the car. The cleaning lady stopped him in the carpark to ask what time they were leaving. She didn't want to go in to clean, until after they had gone.

Minutes later, he returned and grabbed what was left of their luggage.

They left the apartment for the last time. Clara left the key in the door as instructed and they all walked to the car.

With that, Kevin started the car and they drove away. They were upset to be leaving but knew they would be back. William looked over his shoulder as they progressed down the road. A tear rolling down his eye, he waved out of the rear window. The little black body of the cricket, sat on the wall, waving his antennae, bidding them farewell.

The drive back to the airport was quiet. Neither of them said a word. They didn't want to. They just watched the scenery go by.

Eventually the airport came into sight. Kevin pulled into the hire car centre and switched the engine off.

With the bags retrieved from the boot. They made their way into the terminal. Kevin dropped the keys back at the kiosk and took back his deposit.

They checked in and walked through to the departure lounge. Within an hour, they were sitting on the plane and preparing for take-off. A few cheerful passengers were sitting a few rows behind them. They couldn't see why they would be happy to leave. They weren't.

Their journey back was just a blur. The only thing they wanted to do was, to get home and settle in.

William wanted to write down the story of his holiday and was eager to get started.

As soon as the front door was opened. William rushed indoors and up the stairs to his bedroom. Kevin and Clara didn't see him for almost two hours, when he finally came down with a notebook in his hands.

"what's the pad for?" Kevin asked.

William smiled "I want to write about the holiday." And sat at the dining table and began to write.

For the remainder of the afternoon, Kevin and Clara would unpack the suitcases and get washing done.

"when do you think the Doctor call?" she asked him.

"that reminds me "and he rushed into the hallway.

Clara heard a beep as Kevin turned off the answer machine. Four messages in and she could hear the familiar voice of Doctor Parker.

"good afternoon. Doctor Parker here! I know your away. So, as soon as you receive this message, I would like you to ring my office. We have the results."

Clara's heart sunk. The call she was dreading came while they were away. She walked into the hallway; her eyes saddened by the message. "I will call him now" she called out and she picked up the phone and dialled.

Kevin walked through to the kitchen to make some tea.

Moments later Clara walked in. tears streaming down her face.

"what's the matter sweety? What's up?" he begged her.

Sobbing and trying in despair to hold back the tears "he got the results back. It's not good. He wants us in tomorrow, with William."

"oh god!" and he propped himself against the counter. After, what turned out to be an amazing holiday, they had returned to chaos.

The rest of the evening remained silent. Kevin and Clara had both agreed, that they wouldn't tell William and Charlotte although they would have to take William with them to the hospital. They had rung Sarah's parents and asked if it was ok for Charlotte to go round, which they were happy to do.

Dinner was quiet. They ate and they went to bed without saying hardly a word.

The morning came quickly. By eight o'clock the children were dressed.

Kevin and Clara were out of bed, dressed and in the kitchen making breakfast. While they sat in bed, they discussed what they were going to do and if they would tell the children. they agreed not to. They felt it was best to enjoy what they had for as long as the children were there.

Sarah's parents arrived, and Charlotte left for the day. Her and Sarah had a lot of catching up to do. With her gone, Kevin called William down and they were ready to go. William skipped out of the door with his notebook in his hands. He wanted to show the nurse and Doctor his tale of the holiday.

Once at the hospital, they slowly walked down to the Doctors department. Again, as always, they registered their arrival at the reception and sat waiting to be called through. They were sitting in the same seats as they had the first time they were there. Clara wasn't fearful of looking out of the window, where she had seen the cricket. it was almost a distant memory to her.

"Dwyer!" the receptionist called. She remembered them. She didn't even get up from behind her desk to advise them of where they needed to go. She had assumed they knew.

The closer to his office they got the more nervous Clara became.

Kevin knocked on the door.

"come in!" the Doctor called out from inside the office.

He pushed down on the handle and pushed open the door. By his desk, sat the Doctor, an awkward smile on his face.

"hello. Come in!" and he motioned to the chairs.

They entered and sat down.

"how are you William?" he smiled and ruffled his hair.

"I'm good thank you Doctor" he replied. "we've been on holiday!" he added.

"and did you have a lovely time?"

"yeah, it was amazing. We did so much!"

"good. Can you come up on to the bed?" "of course," and He jumped up, swung his feet round.

The Doctor stood up and walked over to William. He began to examine the area of William's head that he took the biopsy from.

"that's healed perfectly and no scar. Brilliant! As you know we took a biopsy of tissue from William's brain" Kevin and Clara both nodded.

"the samples went to be checked. Now this is where the weird part comes in!"

Kevin looked confused. "what weird part?"

The Doctor sat back down. "the sample was received. They did the full works on it and concluded, based on the sample that he had PML. They were ninety eight percent certain." Clara's heart felt tight. She thought she was going to have a heart attack.

"how is that weird?"

"I left you the message on your answer phone and three days later we were contacted by the department that did the tests. They ran them again and found there were no traces of PML at all. it was perfectly clear. I went down to the department to confirm it. I saw it with my own eyes."

Clara sat back in her chair. "so, it's gone?"

"from what we could see, yes! We looked at the samples over and over again. The virus was there, then it was gone. It was as if it was never there in the first place. We even sent the samples to other hospitals to examine. We have never seen anything like this before!"

Clara had calmed down. "so, he hasn't got it?"

"to be honest Mrs Dwyer, it's almost as if William never had it in the first place. All the blood work came back the same."

Fear had now been replaced with joy. William was clear of the virus. She wasn't sure how, the same as the Doctor and the hospital didn't.

"did you hear that William. Your fine!"

William looked at Clara "Charlotte told you, they were there to help."

Clara sat back in the chair. Kevin took hold of Clara's hand.

Clara's emotions, went from fear, to joy, then to confusion. Was it a mistake by the hospital or had the crickets helped him? She looked at Kevin. All he could do was smile back. "he's cured!" she softly said.

Kevin nodded. "if it's gone. Does that mean he can be discharged?"

"it certainly does."

They sat a moment, letting the news sink in.

"if anything, else happens, let us know immediately."

"of course, we will" and Clara beckoned William off the bed and to her side.

The Doctor walked round the bed towards them and held out his hand.

"thank you for coming in. I'm glad it's all over!"

"so are we!" Kevin replied as they turned and walked towards the door.

"I think tonight is pizza night tonight, little dude" he said to William as he lifted him up onto his shoulders.

They got into the car and left the hospital.

Behind them, turning to black vapour was Williams little friend. His antennae waving side to side before they vanished for good.

The End

Printed in Great Britain
by Amazon